A Quest for Victory

Britt Richards

ISBN-13: 978-1-7369053-2-6

To Bear, who proved to me that I can be victorious in writing a novella with an infant attached to me.

Table of Contents

Prologue-Nike
Chapter 1-Nike
Chapter 2-Nike
Chapter 3-Bellerophon
Chapter 4-Nike
Chapter 5-Bellerophon
Chapter 6-Bellerophon
Chapter 7-Nike
Chapter 8-Bellerophon
Chapter 9-Nike
Chapter 10-Nike
Chapter 11-Bellerophon
Chapter 12-Nike
Chapter 13-Bellerophon
Chapter 14-Nike
Chapter 15-Bellerophon
Chapter 16-Nike
Epilogue-Bellerophon
Glossary
Acknowledgement
About the Author
Other Books by Britt Richards

CHAPTER ONE

Prologue-Nike

The scent of burning ground and blood was still strong in the air as I walked the battlefield, looking for those that needed to be finished off or saved. My ears were still filled with the clanging of swords and shields, and Kronos' screams were still echoing off of Olympus and the surrounding valley. Zeus and the others had managed to capture him and were binding him to Tartarus at this very moment.

This was my first war, and I knew deep down, that these battles against the Titans would not have been won had it not been for my help. I've been dubbed "the Goddess of Victory," by my fellow Olympians, and I think I could get used to the title, though not in any sort of vain way.

"Nike!" My mother's near hysterical shriek catches me off guard, and I nearly trip over a limb of some creature I do not recognize.

"Quickly!" My father's usually steady voice, now trembling, calls out.

I run to the end of the battlefield, where my parents are waiting at the tree-line. They each take one of my hands, and then we are gone, flying through time and space until we halt abruptly and are back in the here and now. I breathe in the comforting scent of olive wood burning in the hearth of our home, glad that I'm surrounded with shiny white marble instead of blood and gore.

My mother, Styx, with her milky-white skin, obsidian black hair, and eyes as dark as night, looks significantly paler than I've ever seen her. As for my stoic father, Pallas, I've noticed that his golden olive complexion is pale as well, and he tugs nervously at his tawny brown beard. They're both shaking. As I go into my bedchambers to change out of my bloodied armor, I can hear them muttering something about a growing threat.

I emerge from my chamber, in a fresh, white pelops, in time to hear my mother say, "We have to do this, Pallas. For her safety."

"That *malákas* Zeus! Wouldn't she be safe with you in the underworld, Styx?"

"I would appreciate it if you would stop talking about me as if I'm not here," I cut in before my mother can answer.

My parents give each other a long glance, before they walk over to me and each take a hand once more. They're both shaking, and a pit grows in my stomach as I see the tears in their eyes. "Nike, we have gotten wind that Zeus may be plotting to use you and your power to establish his rule over the rest of us," my father begins.

"We know how close you two are, but his lust for power grows by the day, and your friendship will mean nothing to him. Your father and I have figured out a way to keep you safe. It's only temporary, but we have no other choice."

"You sound as though you're sending me away," I grin, but my grin falters as a single tear slides down my father's face. "You *are* sending me away."

"It's only temporary," Mother sniffs, trying to control her emotions.

Before I can say anything, the two of them pull me into an

all-encompassing embrace. They mumble something incoherently in a dialect of Greek I am unfamiliar with. "*Chaíre,* Nike," is the last thing I hear my father say.

And then there was nothing but black and my consciousness. I was floating in an abyss of endless night. There was nothing and I was no one. I was completely and utterly alone.

CHAPTER TWO

Nike

Time is meaningless here. I do not know if I've been in this dark abyss for mere hours or endless years. The only thing I am certain of is a deep sense of loneliness. Sometimes I muse over how long I've been in this void, but I try not to linger on those thoughts for long. I've known neither hunger nor thirst since arriving here. My body has not touched the ground; I'm simply suspended in the air. I find that I can speak, and if anyone could hear me, they would think I have gone insane with how often I talk to myself, though I just don't want to lose my voice entirely.

And I dream, both when I'm asleep and while I'm awake. At first, the dreams saddened me, but now they are the lifelines I hold onto, my hope that someday I will be freed from this void and be able to live them out. I want to find a love like my parents have, one that is timeless and pure. What would it be like to have a family and a home of my own? Sometimes, I imagine that I'm back in my bedchambers, my soft, down mattress supporting me as I sleep. I never knew such a simple luxury would be something I would miss so dearly.

Sometimes in my dreams, I can feel the sun's warmth on

my face as I soar through the sky around Olympus, the cool winds ruffling my feathers. But when I wake, my wings refuse to unfold, remaining carefully tucked against my back, as if they were a delicate limb in need of protecting instead of my strongest asset.

My blood screams for battle, or, at least an intense training round with my *xiphos*. I was not made for idleness, I was made for warfare and fighting. Oftentimes, I find myself reliving the battle against the Titans, seeing every strike I made. To fight away boredom and despair, I create battle strategies, both offensive and defensive, that live in the recesses of my mind for later use. I dream of weapons I have mastered, and weapons that I want to master. Oh, how I wish I could just put my feet on the ground, run through the grass, and hurl my javelin as far as it will go.

I also find I miss the mundane, like polishing my armor and sharpening my blades. Fates, I even miss cleaning my bedchambers and making my bed. And what I wouldn't give for some honey glazed prawns and some cheesecake. Just to taste a fig or an olive once more would be absolutely divine. Aside from flying and weapons, food is my favorite thing in this world.

My thoughts are interrupted as a bright white light begins to fill my void. It's not the same kind of light as the sun that Apollo pulls across the sky on his chariot, nor is it warm, and it hurts my face. I feel an uncomfortable tugging sensation on my body, and them I'm flying through space and time. Suddenly, I burst back into being, no longer in the abyss and try to take in my surroundings.

A man with dark, wavy brown hair and bronzed skin stands about 10 *podes* away from me, his mouth agape. In his hand is the head of some kind of female monster. Her head is green and her hair is replaced with snakes that are still hissing despite the fact that they are dying and blood is oozing from the severed neck. I turn my head, though the movement feels abnormal. On the ground is the body of the creature, sans head, and all around the cavern I've found myself in, are stone statues of men and women. She must have been a gorgon.

I turn my head back to the man and take a step forward, nearly falling on my face. "Who are you?"

The man's bronzed skin pales as his eyes widen even more. "You can speak?"

I narrow my eyes in confusion. "Of course I can speak. Now answer the question."

He shakes himself as he slides the head of the gorgon into a satchel. "My name is Perseus, son of Zeus and Danaë. I was sent here on a quest to kill the gorgon Medusa, who has been turning people into stone for years. Who, may I ask, are you?"

My blood runs cold at the mention of Zeus, the man I once considered a friend, whom my parents believed was my enemy, the reason I have been away. I shake my head. "I am no one of importance. How did I get here, Perseus?"

Perseus runs a hand through his hair before answering. "I had just severed the gorgon's head when a flash of bright light appeared and you sprang forth from her head. Fates, please tell me you aren't Medusa in another form."

I can't help but laugh at that as I shake my head once more. "I am not. But, why are you looking at me like that? Do I have blood on my face?"

He looks at me with a flush of embarrassment as I try to lift my hand to my face, but nothing happens. I look down and gasp in horror as I see two pure white legs with hooves. "I take it this is not what you're supposed to look like?" Perseus grins awkwardly.

"No. How do I leave this cavern?"

"There's only one way in and out, so just follow the path

behind me."

I nod my thanks and run past him. My gait feels weird, and it feels like I have four legs instead of two. As I emerge from the cave, I close my eyes and pray to the gods that my wings are still there and work the muscles. They immediately unfurl and I breathe a sigh of relief as I launch myself into the sky and fly as fast as I can away from the cavern, not knowing where I am, where I should go, or what direction I am actually flying. The sky is beginning to light in soft hues of predawn pink, and I breathe in a large breath of air.

I can see the mountain that Olympus sits on far away in the distance, and I am shocked to see that the landscape has changed drastically since I was last here. My absence must have spanned a couple hundred years at least. I no longer know this place, but I do know that I need to find somewhere safe to figure out what has happened to me, and find out what the state of Greece is and who I can trust.

After flying for a good hour or so, the unmistakable sensation of magic begins to tickle my body as I near a beautiful forest. The closer I get to it, the more intense the sensation is. There can only be one reason why a forest would be shrouded in this much magic: it must be protected by a very powerful god. I'm very tired, and the magic holds no feeling of animosity, so it seems safe to land. Water glimmers ahead as I glide down and land on the shoreline of a lake. The water is a beautiful shade of turquoise, and it smells so crisp and clean.

I take a step closer, taking in a deep breath, unsure of what my reflection will show. Having never had a lack of courage before, I push myself to take the last few steps and look down into the water, which perfectly mirrors my reflection. And there, instead of the womanly figure I remember with a crisp white pelops and perfectly braided golden hair, stands a massive white horse with giant white wings still outstretched from its body. *My* body.

Shakily, I dip my head and drink deeply from the water. Then I back up, look around until I spot a soft clump of grass, and head over to it. Wearily, I fold my legs beneath me and lay down. Sleep comes quickly, and I don't even try to fight it as tears fall from my eyes and drip down my long face. The face of a horse, not a goddess.

CHAPTER THREE

Nike

The soft sunlight through the morning mist stirs me from sleep. I shake my body and send dew drops flying everywhere, and I can't help the small giggle that escapes my mouth. For so long I have dreamed of having some sort of of sensation back instead of the monotony of floating in the utter darkness. And while this body I'm trapped in is far from what I had wanted, at least I'm back in my world and out of the void. My stomach gurgles, and for the first time in, Fates only know how long, I feel hungry.

Making my way over to the lake, I drink a bit of water to satiate my dry throat, but I can't help but be repulsed as I look at the grass and mull over whether or not I should try it. Horses eat grass, so it should taste fine, right? Wrong. As soon as I bite into the lush greenery, I am filled with regret and spit it out instantly.

"I've never seen a horse spit out grass before," a laugh comes from behind me.

I whirl around as fast as my four legs will allow me to find a woman sitting on a boulder watching me. Her unruly dark brown hair frames her olive colored eyes, which are alight with mirth as she grins.

"Come to think of it, I've never seen a horse with wings, either. And I know of all creatures. But you're not just any horse, are you?" She goes on, not seeming to be bothered by the fact that she's talking to what must seem like a wild animal.

"Er, no, I'm not," I managed to say.

The woman doesn't seem surprised in the least that I can speak. She jumps off of the boulder and makes her way toward me. I notice then that she has a bow and a full quiver of arrows strapped across her back, as well as a spear, a sibyna, if I'm not mistaken. Something about her seems so familiar, yet I can't quite place why. However, the power emanating off of her is unmistakable; she is the goddess that controls this forest.

"Goddess," I greet her, dipping my head low.

She raises an eyebrow. "Goddess? Artemis, if you please. I hate formalities. And if I'm not mistaken, you are also a goddess. Though this is a strange bodily manifestation."

My head snaps up at her name. "Artemis!" No wonder she looks so familiar. We had started to become friends, before the battle. Before my parents sent me away... "It's me, N—" I begin, then snap my mouth shut before I can give myself away.

While I could probably call her a friend, she *is* a daughter of Zeus, and her loyalties are probably to him. I don't know if what was happening when I was sent away has been resolved, and if they haven't, I can't have him finding me.

"I recognize your voice, but I'm sorry, I can't place it. What were you about to say?"

"I'm sorry, Artemis. I can't reveal who I am... Zeus—"

She holds up a hand. "My father and I are not on speaking terms right now. He granted me dominion over this forest and agreed to my terms of not being forced into a marriage, yet every few decades he tries to push me into getting married. And this last time he was especially insistent. So I'm giving him the cold shoulder until he apologizes." Artemis examins her nails and picks some dirt out from under them, a sour look on her face.

I couldn't help but laugh. "Well, as long as you swear to keep my identity a secret…"

Artemis grins at me and crosses her heart. "My lips are sealed."

"I'm Nike, and I don't know how in Olympus I ended up with the body of a winged horse."

"Nike!" She squeals and throws her arms around me. "I knew your voice was familiar. Fates, you've been missing for centuries! What happened?"

Before I can respond, my stomach gurgles loudly once more. "Do you, by chance, know where I can obtain something more… appetizing to eat?"

Laughing, she nods her head and gestures for me to follow her. "Tell me everything on the way back to my house. We have so much to catch up on."

I am relieved to be in a safe, comfortable place. Artemis' home, like any immortal's, is built for a large being, and so, even in this body, I fit inside. The gods are thrice the size of mere men, and being that I am a goddess, albeit in a horse's body, I'm also about thrice the size of a normal horse. She prepared a soft bed of hay and blankets for me near the hearth and made sure I ate my fill of bread and honied figs. I told her what had happened after the final battle against the Titans, and her brow furrowed when I told her how I was pulled back into this realm.

"I've figured it out!" She yells from her bedchamber before striding out, holding up a piece of parchment. "When your parents sent you into the void for your protection, they used the ancient language of the Titans to do so. If my theory is correct, they may have mispronounced one of the words, which placed you under a curse. A harmless one, thankfully, but it would explain why you're not in your normal form."

"That would make sense," I reply as I scan the parchment, which shows some translations of the old Titan language into Greek. "But how do I escape it?"

Artemis leans her forehead against mine, and I can feel her power buzz. She pulls back and purses her lips as she rolls her eyes. "How stereotypical. It seems that the curse requires you to go on a quest, and it wants you to learn something, but I can't figure out what."

"A quest? What kind of quest?"

She shrugs. "All I was able to glean is that you must help a son of Poseidon and learn true courage. I don't know when this quest is to take place, though. In the meantime, we need to give you a name, since we can't have everyone knowing that Nike has been found. If my father wasn't such a *vlaka*..."

"You don't know who the son of Poseidon is?"

Artemis laughs heartily. "Poseidon has... many children.

Much like my father. I don't know which one it is, but I have a feeling it'll be revealed before too long."

"Do you have any suggestions on what to call me?" I ask, because while I am good at a great many things, I am not good at coming up with names.

"How about… Pegasus?"

"I like it!"

"Pegasus it is, my beautiful friend. And while we await whatever quest the curse requires of you, you are welcome to stay here. You will be protected in my forest, along with all of my animals that live here."

For the first time in a long time, I feel like I can finally breathe again. My eyes well up with tears of gratitude, but I can't find the words to thank her, so I just nod. Artemis smiles at me, then grabs her *sibyna*.

"I hope you don't mind, but I need to go hunt down a rogue boar. Feel free to snack or nap, or whatever you like. Tonight, if it's not to strange for you, we shall feast on wild boar to celebrate your return!"

With that, she breezes out the door. I smile as I watch her run silently through the trees until she disappears. While I am unsure of what this quest I'm supposed to go on will be, I am so grateful to no longer be alone.

CHAPTER FOUR

Bellerophon

A loud rap comes from my door, dragging me out of my way too short nap. I'd barely been home for three hours, and all I wanted was to sleep for the rest of the day; I am exhausted. The knock comes again, and I groan as I stretch and reluctantly swing my feet out of bed and stand up. "Alright, alright! I'm coming!"

I yank my door open, prepared to give whoever was interrupting my rest a piece of my mind, but stop short when I see the young sea nymph girl trembling and looking extremely nervous. "I'm sorry, Prince Bellerophon," she squeaks. "His majesty, King Poseidon, requests your presence immediately."

Of course he does. "Thank you…"

"Crisa," the girl supplies with a small smile.

"Thank you, Crisa. Is he in the throne room or his personal study?"

"He is in his study, your highness." With that, the nymph turns and scurries away.

My father always has such impeccable timing. I run a hand through my hair, and with a sigh, I walk toward his study. The magnificent castle under the sea is my favorite of my father's estates, and I love to admire all of the mother of pearl detailing in the hallways. Without knocking, I stride into the study to see my father sitting at his desk and my "aunt" Athena sitting across from him.

"You requested my presence?" I drawl as I take the empty seat by my aunt. I was trying not to sound too annoyed, but I was exhausted and just wanted to go back to sleep.

Poseidon sighs as he looks at me. "Bellerophon, how is it that you always get yourself into such messy situations?"

"He's *your* son," Athena laughs and gives him a pointed look.

"What kind of messy situation?" I have no idea what he's talking about.

"I received a missive from King Iobates of Lycia this morning," my father holds up a letter and stares daggers at me with his deep, ocean blue eyes. "He claims that you cornered his daughter, Queen Anteia, wife of King Proetus, while you were visiting his court and tried to kiss her. And he claims that you were flirting with her all evening."

My mouth falls open and I sputter for a moment trying to get the words out. "I did no such thing!"

"Explain yourself, then."

I take a deep breath as I rub my face in exhaustion. "I did not flirt with her or anyone else during my time in their court. However, the night in question a grand feast was held, and I told Queen Anteia that she looked lovely that evening, and I said the same to all of the noblewomen that were introduced to me. It was the polite thing to do. I also danced one dance with her, as I did with the rest of the noblewomen. As I was heading back to my chambers, *she* cornered *me* and tried to kiss *me*!"

Shuddering at the memory, I roll my eyes and continued. "I immediately put my hands up and asked her what in the world she was doing. She told me that after I'd flirted with her that evening, that she figured she would repay me with a kiss. I very plainly told her that she's a married woman and I'm not that kind of man. She responded that she was that kind of woman and no one had to know."

"It's nice that your son doesn't take after *you* in that regard," Athena winks at Poseidon, who grumbles and rolls his eyes.

"Anteia pouted and tried to hold me there but I extricated myself, returned to my chambers, packed my things, and left immediately. And here I am. She must have told her husband and father that I tried to kiss her since I rejected her advances."

"I see," my father begins before pausing and rubbing his face much in the same manner I had done earlier. "The missive does say that Iobates received word from Proetus about your supposed betrayal. Proetus wanted to hunt you down that very night and kill you, but dared not violate xenia."

I had never been more grateful for the laws of hospitality in all of my life.

"However, King Iobates has no such restrictions. He is demanding that you are turned over to him for execution. According to his laws and customs, your head belongs to him."

My heart felt like it dropped into my stomach and I can feel myself blanche. I had done nothing wrong, and now it seems as though my life is null and void. "Father, you aren't actually considered letting this mortal demand my life from you, are you?" My father is one of the three strongest gods, and as a Demi-god, I was a step above that of a mortal. No one should be demanding anything from the King of the Sea.

Poseidon grins at me, and the kindness in his eyes makes me smile back. "No, son, I am not letting him demand anything from me, but I am going to concede to his alternate request, in an attempt to have you learn a lesson."

I breathe a sigh of relief, knowing there was something on the table other than my life.

"Instead of your head, King Iobates will accept the head of the legendary Chimera, a strange and viscous beast that has been terrorizing the nearby countryside of Caria. I think he's hoping the the beast will kill you, but I have every confidence in your skill."

"My nephew is somewhat of a mighty warrior," Athena puts in. "And with a quest of this magnitude, I think it's fitting that I gift you some armor. It'll be in your chambers when you return there from our meeting."

I smile gratefully at her before turning back to my father. "I have a long journey ahead of me, and could use a companion. May I take one of your horses with me on my quest?"

Poseidon furrows his brow and shakes his head rapidly. "Absolutely not! I will not have you taking one of my precious babies into danger."

"But you'll let me go into danger?"

He grins sheepishly at me. "Yes."

"Well, is that all?" I sigh, wanting my bed.

"Yes, you're dismissed, son. I will have the servants prepare a pack for you before you head out."

I nod, then head out of his steady and back down the hall toward my chambers. As promised, a beautiful set of armor is waiting for me when I open my door. The gold gleams in the firelight from my fireplace, and the expert craftsmanship was definitely that of Hephaestus. At least I would have the protection of this magic-infused armor from my cousin. Feeling restless and unable to fall asleep, I take out my favorite *dory,* a seven-foot long spear with a leaf-shaped head, and start to sharpen it.

A knock comes at my door, and before I can tell the guest to come in, the door opens and Athena walks in.

"Bellerophon, how are you holding up?"

I set my *dory* down and pat the space beside me on the bed. "I'm nervous, and you know I do my best fighting from a horse, but if father won't let me use one of his, then I'm basically a sitting duck. He has yet to gift me my own."

"He is a stubborn man. If you give me a day or two, I will consult with Artemis. She may have an animal companion that would be willing to assist you on your quest. I'm sure you could learn to fight from the back of a great bear or something."

"I would appreciate any help I can get, Aunt Athena."

"Then it's settled. I'll return in a couple days. Until then, rest, eat well, and train."

She hugs me before hurrying out of my room. I am grateful for her help, and just hope that it will be enough. As a Demigod, I am harder to kill than a mortal, but I can still die. And the Chimera, being a beast of legend with powerful magic, wasn't going to be easy to defeat. One wrong move and I'd be a goner. Exhaustion finally hits me, and sleep takes me before my head hits my pillow.

CHAPTER FIVE

Nike

Flying has always been one of my favorite things to do, and while the exercise feels different with me in this horse body, it still feels like freedom. I fly through and just above Artemis' forest, the fresh air is exhilarating, and I can't help but laugh. Several small creatures are startled by my sudden appearance in the air, but several birds take the opportunity to play, weaving all around me in the sky. It's been a long time since I've been able to play with the birds, and I try not to cry as I turn and make my way back toward Artemis' house.

I hope my parents are alright. I'm sure they miss me just as much as I miss them, but Artemis and I both agreed that we can't alert them to my presence yet, just in case what they fear from Zeus is still a possibility. Even after all this time, I can't quite figure out why they were so fearful. Even if he did want to use me for some tyrannical takeover, he'd have to beat me first. And while I am not one to brag, it's unlikely he'd be able to match my skill in any form of fighting. He'd have to bring me to my knees with one of his lightening bolts, which I don't believe he would be coward enough to do.

Landing outside of Artemis' house, I take a long drink from a bowl she placed outside for me and settle my wings tight against my back. I wouldn't want to knock anything over and break something with them. As I step inside, a familiar voice meets my ears, and again I find myself doing everything in my power not to cry. There, at the table talking with Artemis, is my oldest friend. She was my friend, even before Zeus.

Athena hasn't changed a bit, except something about her seems even more wise than when I was sent away. Her sparkling blue eyes seem just as full of mirth as ever, and they widen at the sight of me. I want so badly to run over and throw my arms around her, but I don't have any arms, and she's also Zeus' daughter. There's no way she would abandon her loyalty to him, because as far as I know, he doesn't pressure her into things like he tries to do with Artemis.

"Ah, Pegasus! You arrived back just in time," Artemis grins at me. "It appears the answer we've been seeking, has come to find you instead."

Athena stands, brushing a stray strand of her dark brown locks out of her eyes. "I'm Athena, Goddess of Wisdom and Warfare."

"I'm Pegasus," I bow with my front legs and stoop my head.

"No need to bow," she laughs. "You are clearly a goddess of some sort yourself..

"Tell her!" Artemis is barely containing her excitement.

I try to raise and eyebrow, but the action doesn't really work on my horse face. Athena takes her seat once more and I awkwardly sit on my rear haunches at the table where Artemis has graciously put a plate of *teganites* and figs drizzled in honey for me. She sources everything from her forest or the local village just outside of the forest, a place she says Demeter is especially fond of, so they always have the best and most plentiful crops.

With a twinkle in her eye, Athena turns to me. "I am going

to assume, based on what my sister has told me, that you don't know many people from the present, as you were sent away sometime in the past. Correct?"

I nod, and she continues. "Poseidon has a son, well, actually, he has a lot of sons. But the one I am most fond of is named Bellerophon. I refer to him as my nephew. He has, let's just say, gotten himself into a sticky situation in which he needs to slay the legendary Chimera or be killed himself in payment to King Iobates of Lycia. This is not a quest that he should go out on by himself, and he asked for a companion of sorts. Poseidon won't let him take one of his prized horses, so I offered to ask Artemis if she had a creature in her forest that would be willing to go with him. She suggested you. Will you help my nephew, Pegasus? Please."

I had heard of the chimera before being banished to the void. It was a fearsome creature, and not easily slain. Even as a demigod, this man would have a very hard time slaying the beast on his own. And this must be the quest that will free me from my curse. There really is no other choice. "I will help him, Athena. Under the condition that he treats me as an equal."

"Thank you, Pegasus! Anything you need for the quest, I will pay for Hephaestus to make. He is my next stop before I return to Poseidon's domain and let Bellerophon know."

"With Pegasus, *victory* will surely be on his side," Artemis grins, emphasizing the word "victory."

I roll my eyes at her before turning back to Athena. "Have him meet me where the Spring of Pirene meets the lake. I will await his arrival there."

While I am usually fully confident in my skills to assist whoever needs my help, I'll admit that I'm nervous about this quest. I have the body of a horse, so I am useless when it comes to the actual fighting. Before Athena departed, she said that this young man, Bellerophon, would meet me in three days. Which gives me two and half days to practice maneuvers. So here I am, flying through the forest doing a training regimen that she and Artemis helped me come up with.

I bank right and halt myself in the air with my wings outstretched, to allow someone on my back to fight on that side. Then I bolt straight up into the sky before nosediving towards the ground and pulling up and banking left at the last moment. I try out all sorts of maneuvers, banking this way and that, varying my speed and the ways in which I hold my wings. It is exhausting, as this body is much heavier than my normal body. And these are just the exercises in the air, I haven't even attempted the ones on the ground.

Even though I'm not in my true form, I feel much more confident in the sky since I still have my wings and it's something I can do without legs. But the thought of learning how to essentially *be* a horse fills me with embarrassment and trepidation. I cannot under any circumstances let this would be hero see me fall flat on my face with all four legs splayed out in every direction. So far I can barely walk on all four hooves, much less run. And this battle will require that I be light on my hooves and able to turn on a *tetartemorion*. There will be no room for mistakes. Because if I am too slow or I choose the wrong maneuver... we will both die. And I simply can't have that.

I train for hours, not bothering to stop for lunch or dinner. It's easy for me to ignore the rumblings of hunger, because even though I am not training with one of my favorite weapons, the act of exerting my body to prepare for battle is as familiar as an old friend, and a routine I am used to. In fact, it is the most normal and comforting thing I've been able to do since reemerging from the void. It's not until I hear my name being called that I finally come to a halt and start walking back toward Artemis' home.

She's waiting for me at the edge of the forest where it meets the clearing her home sits in, and she seems worried. "What's wrong?" I ask.

"You've been gone for hours, Nike! I was worried something had happened to you."

"I'm sorry, Artemis. I lost track of time. Being able to train again is such a balm to my soul, that I didn't think about the fact that you would be waiting for me."

The worried look melts into a smile. "I understand completely. Whenever I have to go spend an extended amount of time on Olympus, and am unable to run through my forest and hunt, kills me a little on the inside every time. And when I finally get home and my bare feet bound the earth as I sprint the paths with my bow on my back… that's when I feel fully alive."

I can't help but grin at her. "That is exactly how I feel when I fly and train. I just with I had my *xiphos*."

CHAPTER SIX

Bellerophon

It's been three days since my father informed me of this task I must complete. I feel like all I've done is gather supplies, practice fighting, go over strategies, and pace. So much pacing. It's what I'm doing now, pacing my room, waiting for Athena to return, and hoping against hope that she was able to find some sort of companion for me. It'll be a lonely journey, but just having an animal companion to talk to, even if they can't respond, would be better than nothing.

How on Olympus did the truth of what happened get so skewed? Queen Anteia must be the super vindictive type, if she went to her husband and father and lied to them about what happened so they'd call for my death. She would have known what the laws demand, and was too eager to see it done. And all I had tried to do was the honorable thing. I pause my pacing to grab my last empty satchel and stuff some candles, flint, and a knife into it. Before I can resume my pacing, my door flies open and I turn to find Athena gliding into my chambers.

Her warm expression and calm demeanor calms my worries for the time being and I smile at my aunt. "You're back!"

"Of course I'm back. I apologize for taking so long, but I had several stops to make."

"No need to apologize. Did you find a companion for me?"

Athena's smile stretches across her entire face. "I found the most perfect companion for you, Bellerophon. She has agreed to help you, but on one condition."

"An animal that is able to communicate conditions? I know Artemis has a special connection to animals but I didn't know it went *that* deep."

"Let's just say that with this being, looks can be deceiving. I have a theory on who she truly is, but since she did not want to share it with me, I will keep my suspicions to myself."

"Alrighty then. What is her condition?"

"She wants you to treat her as an equal during this quest, and I strongly advise that you heed her wishes and her wisdom."

"I will. She must be able to speak then?" Athena nods and I continue, "That's a relief. I won't spend the whole journey talking to myself."

"No, you won't," she laughs. "She asked that you meet her tomorrow where the Spring of Pirene meets the lake in Artemis' forest."

"Tomorrow! There's no way I can make it there on foot. It would take me no less than a week."

"Good thing your father is the God of the Sea and has agreed to open a portal for you."

So he's not leaving me all on my own after all. I will have to thank him before I go for sure. "Perfect. Can you at least tell me what my companion looks like?"

"I could, but I'm not going to. I want your reaction to seeing her to be genuine."

I sigh but Athena only laughs before she walks over and embraces me tightly. "Any parting words of wisdom for me,

Goddess of Wisdom?"

"Trust your companion, she will not let you down. Study the chimera and its patterns before you attack. There is no hurry, Iobates will get the chimera's head when he gets it, so take your time. Promise me you will heed my words."

"I will, Athena, I promise."

"Good," she brushes away a few tears as she steps back and reaches for a pack I had not noticed her leave on the floor when she entered my room. "A couple more parting gifts. Use them well. I'm afraid I won't be able to see you off; my father has requested my presence. I love you, little nephew. *Chaíre.*"

With a spin, she was gone. *Chaíre, Athena,* I think before opening the pack. The first thing I pull out is a very large bridle made entirely of woven gold thread. I pull on it and snap the reins, expecting it to break, but it is just as sturdy as the finest leather and snaps like it too. The second thing in the pack takes my breath away.

It is the most beautiful weapon I have ever laid eyes on, and most definitely Hephaestus' handiwork. I've never seen another *xiphos* like it. Not only is this *xiphos* a leaf-bladed variety of the sword, but it's double-edged and gilded, too. I'm speechless. Raising my arm, I test the sharpness of the blade by attempting to shave off a couple of my arm hairs. It has the sharpest blade I've ever come across, and easily removes a whole patch of hair. How embarrassing. I'm glad I didn't try shaving my face with it.

Given that I only have a few hours before I would need to attempt to sleep, I figure now is as good a time as any to practice with my new sword. I head to the armory that doubles as a training ground. I test the balance of my sword, grinning at the flawlessness of it. There are a couple practice dummies, and I get into fighting stance and attack. I push myself for a good hour before pausing for a break. With a bit more thought, I test the sharpness of the blade once more, and it hasn't dulled in the slightest.

"Need a sparring partner?" A familiar voice asks from behind me.

I turn to see my father with one of his favorite blades in hand. He has a goofy grin on his face, and I can't help but grin back at him. While he is just as formidable as his brothers, he is also the kindest and has the best sense of humor. "No trident?" I question him with a raised brow.

"It wouldn't be a fair fight to spar trident against sword. I'd make you tap out in seconds, son," he teases with a wink.

"Fair enough," I chuckle.

"Take your mark,"

No sooner do I get in position than Poseidon is upon me. While the trident is the weapon that acts like an actual extension of his being, he is almost just as adept at using a *xiphos*. He rains blow after blow at me, and it takes me a moment to get my bearings and go from blocking on the defensive to striking on the offensive. I know he's not holding back much for my own benefit, so that I'll be ready to face the chimera. While he refuses to step in too much on my behalf, I know he loves me and doesn't want me to die. Fates, I really don't want to become the chimera's next meal.

I keep up with my father's blows for quite some time, but it doesn't take too long before I'm on my knees, my new *xiphos* several feet away from me, and my father's blade at my throat. "Do you tap?"

I can't help but laugh at the smug grin on his face. "Yes, I tap!"

"Good!" He exclaims, sheathing his sword and holding out a hand to help me up, which I gladly take. "Cause I'm starving. Come on, son. I have a farewell feast waiting for us in the dining hall."

"Don't have to tell me twice!" I pick up and sheath my

own sword before turning toward the door.

Poseidon throws an arm around my shoulders and we walk out of the armory together. I can't remember the last time we did this, and I pray to all of Olympus that I get to do it again.

CHAPTER SEVEN

Bellerophon

Morning comes way too soon, but I know that this quest has been put off long enough. I dress as quickly as I'm able, irritated that I have to *wear* my armor on my way to meet this companion, but hopefully I won't have to wear it for the whole journey. While it fits perfectly and moves as if it's a part of me when I fight, it is not comfortable to wear long-term. All of my packs are waiting for me by the door, but I notice an extra one that wasn't there the night before. I peak inside to find an exorbitant amount of rations, with a honey cake in the shape of a trident sitting on the top of all the wrapped portions. So it would seem my father has left me one final gift, though this seems like way too much food for one person.

Grabbing all of my packs, I shoulder them before sliding my new *xiphos* into its sheath on my belt and leave my room, praying to the Fates that I'll get to return to it someday. I take my time wandering down the hallways that will lead me to the reflecting pool room where my father has opened a water portal for me. I know I'm stalling, but I want to try to memorize my home, since I may perish. The thought makes my stomach sink, but I roll my eyes knowing that if my father or Athena could hear my thoughts, they would never let me hear the end of it for being "dramatic."

The reflecting pool shimmers with my father's power as I approach it, the portal ready for me to step inside. Taking one last look about, I take a deep breath and step into the water. I am immediately sucked into it, and I travel as if I am sliding down some sort of chute. It spits me out with a small burst of water as I land on my rear end on the grassy bank of a beautiful lake. A soft snicker meets my ears as I jump up and brush myself off. I'd always heard about the beauty of the Spring of Pirene, and the tales weren't false. The water s crystalline, the foliage vibrant shades of green, the air sweet with the scents of flowers.

I turn around and freeze as my gaze lands on the most magnificent being I have ever laid eyes on. In the grassy field behind me stands a massive winged horse, as white as the clouds over Olympus, or of the mythical snow that I have never seen. She holds herself proudly as she gazes back at me, and I can see the golden aura emanating from her. This is no mere horse. No, this being is a goddess, and a strong, powerful one at that. The only thing I can think to do in her presence is to bow before her. Before I really know what's happening, I fall to my knees and bow my head in reverence.

"Goddess," I breathe. "My name is Bellerophon, son of Poseidon. I beg for your aid on my journey to slay the legendary chimera."

"Please stand up, Bellerophon, there is no need for this... formality," she says with the most melodious voice I have ever heard.

I do as she says and stand, unable to keep from staring at her. "How should I address you?

"You are correct in that I am a goddess, though this is not my true form. You may call me Pegasus," she says, trying to smile, but grimaces when she can't get her horse mouth to do what she wants. "In any case, I pledge to help you to the best of my ability, and with me, you will be victorious on your quest."

"Thank you, Pegasus!" I exclaim before striding over to her. As a demigod, I am much bigger than mortals, which makes riding a horse difficult since there are few big enough. However, Pegasus is thrice the size of a normal horse, perfect for me. And now that I think about that, I feel a flush creep over my face. This is an actual *goddess*, and here I am thinking of her as if she's *just* a horse. Fates save me, I can't possibly suggest riding on her! I'm going to die from embarrassment before I can even get close the the chimera.

"I apologize," Pegasus says before I can think of something to say. "I don't have a saddle or armor yet, and I've only ever carried Artemis on my back, and that has only happened in the last couple of days while I prepared for you to arrive. Will you be alright bareback while we fly to Hephaestus' workshop?"

I gape at her, completely shocked that she is in fact going to carry me on her back. Not knowing what else to do, I nod, feeling my face go as red as Hephaestus' forge. She snickers again, the sound a bit odd, but she doesn't comment. Remembering my gift from Athena, I set one of my packs on the ground and rummage through it until I find the bridle made of gold and pull it out.

"This was a gift from my aunt, Athena," I explain as I hold it out for her to see.

Pegasus steps closer to me and her eyes roam the bridle. A deep sigh escapes her, but she meets my eyes and nods at me. "I suppose since I am currently a horse, I will have to wear that… bridle. But for the love of the three Fates, please just use it to hold on to. I really don't want to be jerked around."

Unable to help myself, I chuckle at the dismal look she has on her face. She glares at me, then lowers he head. "I promise not to jerk your head around. Besides, you could simply buck me off to my death while we fly if I get on your nerves to much, though I really hope you won't," I say as I gently place the bridle over her head and fasten it.

The gold looks absolutely brilliant over her pure white hair. "Whether I like it or not, water boy, my fate is tied to yours on this quest. I will not be the cause of your death. No, we will save each other."

"W-water boy?" I splutter.

"You are the son of Poseidon, are you not?" Pegasus laughs.

"Well, yes, but I am no water boy."

"If you say so. Now, if you please, I'd like to get going before the morning gets away from us, yes?"

I nod, and work on carefully fastening my packs to her back with rope, which is not ideal, but there is no saddle from which to tie them. She grunts as I cinch the last one a bit too tight, and I mumble a quick apology. I check each pack to make sure they're secure, then softly pat her neck. "May I, uh, mount up?"

"Do you need help?" She asks, and snickers again at my heated cheeks.

I grit my teeth and rub my face. This is going to be a very long quest indeed if I cannot get a grip on my thoughts and feelings. "No, I do not," I nearly growl in annoyance as I swing myself up, remembering to be gentle almost too late, but I manage to catch myself and settle gently onto her back.

"Artemis found it easiest to act as if we are still on the ground when trying to stay balanced," Pegasus begins as she starts to trot.

On the ground? I think to myself, then my eyes widen as her wings unfurl, stretch out, and begin beating on either side of me. And then we are in the air, and I can't help the unmanly squeak that escapes my mouth. I had seen her wings, but it hadn't crossed my mind that we would actually be *flying*.

"Bellerophon!" She yells and I shake myself, realizing she has been trying to get my attention.

"Yes?"

"You're squeezing me too tightly. "

I look down and realize my knees are jabbed into either side of her stomach, and I very carefully release the pressure, and she takes a deep breath. "Thank you. You have nothing to fear. Flying is second nature to me! Enjoy the view!"

And while fear is trying to claw its way into my mind the higher we climb into the air, I can't help but be in awe at the views before me. I can see for miles in all directions, and the vibrant colors of the landscape brings a smile to my face as I take it all in. Never in a million years did I ever think I'd see Greece this way, but here we are. I can only pray to the Fates that I don't fall.

CHAPTER EIGHT

Nike

It is quite an odd feeling to be carrying someone on my back, but it does not overshadow the feeling I get from flying. While it doesn't feel the same as it did when I was in my other body, it feels so freeing. I love the feeling of the wind in my feathered wings. And now that Bellerophon isn't squeezing the air out of my lungs, it's a pretty comfortable flight.

Bellerophon… it's like Aphrodite herself made and sent me the man of my dreams. He seems just a bit taller than I usually am, and has very broad shoulders. He is fit, but not trim, and he has raw strength that doesn't all come from his father. His hair is dirty brown, coming past his ears, and he seems like he wears it messy. He has facial hair, but not a lot, and I happen to find it quite endearing.

It was also very amusing how much he blushed during our initial introduction. While it is strange that I have a whole person riding on my back, it doesn't make near as uncomfortable as it seemed to make him. I am, after all, currently a winged horse. I wonder if he would be more uncomfortable if he found out who I really am, because I slaughtered more creatures during the war than anyone else.

And I know that on a few of those occasions, I was a bit more ruthless than was completely necessary.

We near Hephaestus' forge, and I can see the thick, black smoke billowing out of the chimney. Bellerophon shifts on my back and tightens his grip on the reins, but true to his word, he does not pull on them, just steadies himself. I land as graciously as I can, and turn my head to offer Bellerophon a smile, though I'm sure it looks strange. "Well, how was your first flight?"

"I'm not going to lie... it was rather terrifying," he chuckles and runs a hand through his very mussed up hear in an attempt to tame it. "But it was also the most incredible experience of my life."

"I was a bit nervous the first time I flew when I was a child, but it quickly became the best part of my life."

He nods his head in agreement before dismounting. Standing beside me for a moment, he strokes my neck and straightens out a tangle in my mane. It is such a weird sensation for someone to me *petting* me, but not wholly unwelcome. Though, if horses could blush, I'm sure my face would be as red as blood. Bellerophon seems to remember that I'm not just a horse and his face goes as red as I'm sure mine is under this white hair.

"Sorry," he mumbles as he steps back quickly. "It's hard to remember that you're not just a horse."

I laugh and attempt a shrug, and nearly lose my balance. "It's no big deal. Come on, let's go inside."

Before we can reach the door, it bursts open with a resounding "bang" and a giant of a man, well, god, steps out. His face is disfigured, he has a mechanical arm of some sort, and he walks with a limp. But on his face is the biggest, brightest smile as he holds his arms out wide. "Bellerophon, Pegasus! Welcome to my forge!" Hephaestus greets us.

"Hey, Uncle H!" Bellerophon grins and, and if he were a

child, runs and springs into the god's arms. Hephaestus squeezes him tightly and twirls him around before setting him back on the ground. This man is absolutely enormous, completely dwarfing me as a horse.

"It's nice to meet you, Hephaestus. Did Athena tell you we were coming?" I ask.

"She did indeed. My sister mentioned that you are in need of some tack and armor. Come in, come in! I have a delectable spread prepared, and then we can get to the measurements."

He holds the door open for the two of us and we step inside. Bellerophon leans in and whispers in my ear as we near the table, "Uncle Hephaestus doesn't get many visitors. When he was born, Hera took one look at him, decided he was too ugly, and threw him off of Olympus."

"That's horrible!" I whisper gasp.

"It was. He survived, obviously, and Zeus got him set up down here where he can enjoy some peace and quiet and work on his craft. He may not be the most attractive looking man, but you will not find a kinder, gentler, more hospitable man out there. And he makes a mean roasted lamb!"

On cue, Hephaestus glides in from the kitchen holding a tray with the most delicious smelling roasted lamb I have ever had the privilege of smelling. Smiling and chatting with Bellerophon, he serves the lamb to us with perfectly cooked onions, turnips, and carrots. My mouth waters as I take in the feast before me. For dessert, he produces a platter with honey sesame bars, which he proudly explained that he always add extra pistachios to, various cheeses, fresh honey, and sweet figs.

"Thank you, Hephaestus. I don't know that I have ever eaten this well in my life," I compliment as he begins taking my measurements following our meal. Bellerophon grins at me in approval as he clears the table.

"Oh, you are most certainly welcome. I don't get a lot of

company, and it is always a pleasure when my nephew visits," he says as he writes down the various measurements and sketches some ideas on his wax tablet. "You two should get some rest. Bellerophon knows where his bed is, and I've set up a makeshift stall filled with soft hay over there," he points.

My eyes well with tears at this thoughtful man, and my heart aches that he's so alone in this place. "That is so kind of you. Is there anything I can do to help you? I'm missing hands, obviously, but I am able to hold things quite well with my mouth."

"No, no. You rest! I love my craft, and this forge fills me with joy. When you awaken in the morn, all of your gear will be ready."

I am quite exhausted after the flight, so I nod my head and nuzzle his side, since I can't hug him. As soon as I get my form back, I will remedy that. I find my corner and lay down in the soft hay, curling my legs beneath my body. It doesn't take long for me to drift off to the sound of the two men chatting quietly and the ringing of a hammer on metal.

I awake to the soft light of dawn shining in through the windows. Hephaestus is asleep in a chair by the forge fire, and I can hear Bellerophon snoring from his room. I roll my eyes. If he snores like that every night, we will have to make our camp far from where the chimera lurks or it will hear him and hunt us down. As quietly as I can, I stand, stretch, and make my way outside. I launch myself into the air and fly a ways for some privacy to relieve myself. Finding a stream, I take the opportunity to bathe as best I can as a horse before I head back to the forge.

Stepping back inside, I find a groggy Bellerophon sitting at the table sipping on a steaming mug of what appears to be hot milk and honey. A bowl of it is waiting for me, and I take my place just in time for Hephaestus to waltz in with a plate of fruits and cheese for our breakfast. "Ah, you made it back! I told my nephew that you probably just needed a few moments to yourself, but he was ready to storm out of here to find you. I think he was worried."

Bellerophon grunts and rolls his eyes. "She doesn't have any armor yet, how is she supposed to protect herself?"

"I can protect myself far better than you think, water boy. But thank you for the concern."

Hephaestus spews out a mouthful of milk as he roars with laughter. "Water boy!"

I grin at him and Bellerophon smacks his forehead with his palm.

True to his word, a beautiful, perfectly crafted set of armor and tack are waiting for me when I finish eating. They are made of some sort of metal alloy and gilded in gold. The saddle is soft and supple, and I find that I am not uncomfortable in the slightest, even as Hephaestus cinches it tightly. "Go on," he begins, "Go take a spin with my nephew to see how it feels."

He doesn't have to tell me twice. Rushing back outside, I see that my companion is just as excited as I am, and he swings up into the saddle with ease. I gallop a good *stadion* away from the forge before unfurling my wings and pushing myself up above the ground. While the armor adds extra weight, it's not nearly as heavy as I expected. We glide through the air, Bellerophon whooping with glee. I do a few maneuvers, and am pleased to find that he takes them in stride, mimicking my movements.

We land, and Hephaestus ties our packs onto my new saddle. "Thank you, Hephaestus. It's all so beautiful and fits perfectly."

"You're very welcome, Pegasus. It was my pleasure. Now, you take care of Bellerophon, alright?"

"I will! And when we have succeeded in slaying the

chimera, I will return to see you."

He brushes a tear from his face and embraces me, then Bellerophon. My companion hugs him for quite some time, and I know that he is worried that he won't return from our quest. I feel a sting in my heart, and I firm up my resolve that we will be victorious. I am the goddess of victory, after all. Bellerophon swings up onto my saddle once more, and with one last smile at our gracious host, I lift into the air and turn northwest, toward the chimera, and our destiny.

CHAPTER NINE

Bellerophon

While it is still quite scary, I find that I'm beginning to like flying. It helps that I have a saddle to sit on and stirrups to support my feet. We've been flying for hours, neither of us doing much talking. But we are coming up on sunset, and I'd like to make camp before it gets dark. I reach my hand out and gently pat Pegasus' neck, which I find is slick with sweat and she shutters in exhaustion.

"Pegasus, I think it's time to make camp."

"I... would... agree," she replies, clearly winded.

"It looks like we are coming up on a small clearing with a creek running to the western side."

She nods and banks to the left, angling her body down as she pulls her wings in tight to her body. Before we can hit the ground, she unfurls her wings and we seem to float gently to the grass. No sooner do I slide off her back than she's at the creek with her mouth in the water, drinking deeply. I chuckle and walk up next to her, then bend down to fill up my canteen before taking a long drink myself. Lifting my hands above my head, I stretch up, then stretch down, loosening my stiff muscles.

Pegasus attempts to raise an eyebrow at me before turning

and making her way to the edge of the clearing where the forest meets the grass. She awkwardly lays down, tucking her four legs under her. "Would you mind starting a fire and making dinner?" She asks me. "Since I am unable."

I shrug and head into the trees, being mindful to only take the dead branches off of the ground so as not to upset any dryads that may be in the area. I'd learned my lesson the hard way in my youth, when I'd taken a branch and started stripping the leaves and bark off of it to make a javelin. The woman had lept from the tree faster than I could blink and slapped me hard on the cheek, flung me to the ground, and then retreated back into tree. In the next moment, the tree had sprinted away, leaving me gaping from my spot on the ground.

My father had found the whole thing absolutely hilarious when I told him about it. He'd informed me that it could have been much worse, that the dryad could have killed me, but I'd had my youth on my side, as they were opposed to mortally harming children. The memory makes me smile as I return to where we will camp, and nearly drop my armful of wood when I find Pegasus attempting to set up our tent.

She has a stake in the ground, a hammer in her mouth, and is bent in such an awkward way trying to hammer it down. I simply cannot help myself; I laugh. Loudly. Pegasus looks up at glares at me, and I duck as quickly as I can as the hammer is flung toward my head. "Look, I know how ridiculous it must look to see a horse trying to put up a tent, but you don't have to laugh. I've slaughtered monsters who simply looked at me the wrong way on the battlefield, and normally, I can put up a tent within minutes. Excuse me for trying to be of assistance."

I hold my hands up apologetically. "I'm sorry, it was just a comical sight. I appreciate you trying to help, though. Let me get this fire going and then I'll finish setting up the tent, alright?"

Mumbling something under her breath, she stomps over to our supplies and grabs a pot. I watch her walk back to the creek, chuckling at the way she's still muttering. It is impressive to see her successfully fill the pot and carry it back. I have the fire smoldering as she makes it back to me and sets the pot beside me. "I'll be right back, Bellerophon," she informs me, and before I can ask her where she's going, she's already up in the air and flying away from me.

When I woke up this morning to find her gone, I was quite panicked, but Uncle Hephaestus had talked some sense into me. He'd reminded me that while she was currently in the body of a horse, she was a woman on the inside, and probably wanted some privacy to relieve herself. That had made my face burn again, but I understood completely. She probably just needs a moment to herself right now, and I can't blame her for it. It must be incredibly difficult to no longer have hands, to no longer be in your own body.

I set the pot on top of the fire before rummaging around in my pack for some food. In one of the packages from my father I find four large sea bass, still surprisingly fresh after two days of travel, though I suppose he put some sort of enchantment on them. I take one for myself and gather a handful of turnips and spinach to cook with it. Placing them in the pot, I season them before grabbing a small loaf of bread to eat with my fish once it's done cooking.

It doesn't take long for Pegasus to come back, and she lands lightly beside the fire, careful not to put it out with the wind from her wings. She looks at my food and then up at me, attempting to raise one of her eyebrows. "That doesn't seem like enough food for two people, Bellerophon."

"Uh, I didn't think you would eat it..." I start, feeling my face flush.

"Did you assume that I'd eat grass?"

"Yes?"

If looks could kill, I'm sure I'd be dead. She stares at me as if she would like to run me through with my own *xiphos*. Then it once more dawns on me that she's not truly a horse, and for Fates sake she ate the same meals I did when we were with Hephaestus. I'm such an idiot. "I'm sorry, Pegasus. I keep forgetting... Here, you can have this portion and I'll cook another for myself."

She sighs but giggles a little. "I suppose it is a little ridiculous of me to expect you to remember that I'm a woman when all you see is a horse. Apology excepted, Bellerophon. Do you mind if I call you Bel?" She asks as almost an afterthought.

"Bel?"

"Yeah. Your name is long, so it makes sense to shorten it."

"If you really want to, I suppose it'll do," I chuckle as I serve her the food and turn to make another portion for myself.

"Great!" Pegasus attempts to grin but it looks like a horrible grimace and she shakes her head in frustration. She eats quickly, and then to my surprise, takes off running. I watch her as I eat my own meal, and I can see her weaving through the trees in a very calculating manner. I realize with a start that she's training. After flying us all day, she's not taking this time to rest, but to continue learning to maneuver as a horse.

I watch in awe as she tries various things, like sprinting full steam then hurling herself into the air at the last second before hitting her target. She grabs a stray stick with her mouth and awkwardly jabs at a rotten stump before trying to hurl it like some sort of javelin. Wiping my hands on my tunic, I draw my sword and head to another rotting stump, where I know that no dryad is living within. If she can spend the evening training, then so can I.

"Not too shabby, water boy," I hear as I thrust my sword through the stump in what would be a killing blow to a human. "But your stance isn't fully balanced."

I look over at her and raise a brow. "Excuse me?"

"Your legs need to look more like this," she moves her two front legs awkwardly, but I can see where she's going with the gesture.

Doing as she instructs, I run through my regiment once more, and this time, I feel a bit more force as my *xiphos* drives through the stump. She was right; I felt way more on balance. "Well by the Fates," I breathe.

"Told you. Now, I think it's time we practice together. We need to learn to be in rhythm while fighting, or else the chimera will find us an easy snack."

Nodding in agreement, I grab her saddle and strap it on before climbing into the stirrups. Night is approaching quickly, so I don't think we will have much time, but it's better to get some work in than none. Pegasus surprises me by cantering into the field instead of pushing us into the air. She banks near another tree stump, and I take the opportunity to swing at it. She does this a few times, coming at it from various angles on the ground before launching us into the air, and attacking from above.

By the time darkness starts to fall, we are both heaving in exhaustion. She lands next to our makeshift camp and I relieve her of her tack. "Good work, Bel," she praises as she settles her legs beneath her in our tent.

"You as well," I grin, rolling out my sleeping mat. "Get some rest, we still have a lot of ground to cover tomorrow.

CHAPTER TEN

Nike

We travel for another week before we finally come upon the area the chimera is supposed to be. I land quite a ways off, so that the creature won't smell us and try to make us its snack prematurely. Bellerophon and I setup camp quickly, and since it is still early morning, we have all day to scout. "Bel?" I say as he walks out of the tree canopy carrying an armful of wood for our fire.

"Yeah?" He asks, dropping the wood and running a hand through his tousled hair.

My eyes follow his movements, and I find the action endearing. It takes me a moment to realize he's waiting for me to respond, and I shake my head in a very undignified way and clear my throat. "We should sneak over that hill and scout the chimera. It's important to know our enemy and not go in blind. It's early still, so we can observe its patterns and make our plan of attack."

"A wise suggestion," Bellerophon nods with a smile, though I can tell he's nervous. I wish it was safe for me to just tell him who I am, that he truly has victory on his side. But I can't, not yet.

"We should be alright without our armor, but bring your

sword, just in case. If it smells us and comes near, I'll fly us back to safety."

"Agreed."

I watch as he picks up his sheath and puts the belt around his waist, then rummages around in one of the packs. He pulls out a couple cakes and I try to grin, but it feels weird and I know it must look hideous. Bel sees my face and laughs, and I can feel my skin grow hot. It's utterly embarrassing to try anything human as a horse. He grins sheepishly and holds out one of the cakes he grabbed, and I eat it out of his hand, trying to swallow my embarrassment with each bite. His other hand absentmindedly brushes through my mane, and I wonder if he'd be so bold as to do that if it was my normal head.

It would probably feel wonderful, having his rough, calloused hands work through my hair to gently untangle it. I wouldn't mind it, but I doubt he's developing any sort of attraction for me. He only knows me as a horse, and cannot fathom the woman within. Though, as we've gotten to know each other better on this journey, it may not be too far fetched. The more I learn about him, the more I'm convinced that he must be my soulmate. He has a heart for the people of this country, and others have wronged him, spinning tales about him and twisting the truth.

I can't help but draw parallels to my own life. I love this land, well, the land I once knew, though I suppose it's still the same even though it looks different after all this time. I wouldn't have fought and shed some of my own blood if I didn't. All I want is to defend it, and make sure its people thrive, even if that means someday working against the Pantheon, depending on what I learn of Zeus. I hope it doesn't come to that.

Bellerophon seems to remember himself, and he quickly pull his hand from my mane and turns away. "We should probably get going."

We quietly make our way through the trees and up the hill. Bel drops to his stomach and starts to crawl as we near the top, but that's not something I can physically do, so I crouch down as much as I'm able and continue walking slowly. Reaching the top, I tuck my my legs beneath me and lay down in the grass. Bellerophon crawls toward me, and once he reaches me, sits and rests against my side as we gaze down into the valley below.

Directly beneath us is a cave mouth, and I can smell the scent of beast in the air. There are carcasses in various states of rot scattered all over the valley. Most are animals, like sheep and goats, and I can make out some cattle remains. But then my eyes land on some that are not animal at all, and my stomach twists. I'm no stranger to death, but the war I fought in did not include legendary beasts consuming people as meals. It is truly a horrific sight, and I try to not let my gaze land on those areas in the valley.

I can tell that it's making my companion feel sick on the inside, as he's shaking against my flank. "Easy, Bel. All is well, just try not let your gaze linger. Turn your focus to the landscape and how we might use it to our advantage in this fight."

He lets out a shaky breath and takes in a deep one, calming himself, and in turn, calming me. There is a stream to the north of the cave, and the banks are covered in thick, tall reeds that even I could hide in. To the east is a small copse of trees, but the trees themselves are large and close together. We could hide there as well, but we could also get stuck if we aren't careful. To the west, the valley continues on in a fairly endless expanse of grass, though I know a small village lies several *stadions* away.

An open expanse like that would work to our advantage from the air. I'm about to say as much when an animalistic sound that I can't quite describe comes from below us. We watch in horror as the beast emerges from the cave. I knew by its name that it would be a thing of nightmares, but I was not as prepared as I thought I was for the sight in front of me.

The chimera is at least twice my size, though it could easily be thrice, it is hard to gauge from our vantage point. Its body is that of a lion, and its *main* head is that of a lion as well, and that is where the similarities to that great predator end. From the middle of its back protrudes the head of goat, one that beats and blinks on its own even as the lion head roars before breathing fire over a recently deceased bull and snaps up a large bite. Its underbelly has goat udders, a sight so bizarre that I almost miss its final attribute. Instead of a lion's or goat's tail, the chimera has a giant green snake. The end is a snake head, and I can hear it hissing even from all the way up here.

Bellerophon and I turn to each other, our eyes wide, but we dare not make a sound. My mouth feels dry, and I swallow hard. He must be feeling the same, as his tongue darts out to wet his lips before he takes a deep breath. His eyes hold a measure of fear, but I also see a firm determination in them, and that makes me attempt another smile. In silence, we watch the creature as it devours its meal, then goes to the creek to take a long drink. Its lion head does all of the eating and drinking, though I watch the snake head capture and devour a rodent while it's at the stream.

Once it finishes at the water, we watch as it paces its territory for about an hour before finding a soft patch of grass perfectly positioned under the sun to lay on. I don't know why I find it so strange that this ginormous beast that is mostly a big cat, would act like a normal feline and take a nap in the sun. But that's exactly what it's doing. Occasionally, the goat and snake heads swivel around on alert, and I know that those two could be a detriment to our success if we don't take all three heads into account.

I move my head slightly toward Bel's and whisper as quietly as I can, "I think we are going to have to bring all three of its heads to Iobates. Then there will be no questioning whether the creature is truly dead or not."

"That is a good point," he whispers back.

Inwardly I groan, and pray to the Fates my companion thought to bring some sacks with him. I'm not squeamish in the slightest when it comes to blood and gore, but I glower thinking about my pristine, white flanks being stained red. Not to mention the smell of rot that would emanate off of me.

The beast naps for about two hours, judging by the sun's position in the sky. It awakens and stretches out, and again I find myself surprised at the way it behaves just like a cat. We watch as it prowls its territory once more before it stalks off to hunt. I pity the being it decides to make its next meal. When it leaves our sight, Bellerophon stands and stretches, and I do the same. We walk quietly back to our camp, not daring to talk until we reach it. Bel grabs some cheese and fruit out of a pack and sits next to the pile of wood he'd dropped earlier. He offers some to me and I take it eagerly right as my stomach grumbles loudly.

Bel throws back his head and laughs as it grumbles again. "It's a good thing that didn't happen while we were still on the hill. The chimera would have noticed us for sure."

"It would have been poor timing indeed. Did you see the way the snake head snatched up that rodent?"

"It struck way faster than I thought it could move. We are going to have be very care—"

An animalistic scream resounded throughout the valley and cut him off. Without a word, we both take off toward the chimera's lair. Luckily we remember to crouch before we crest the hill. As I look over the edge, I can see the chimera dragging a wild boar across the valley. It's screaming in agony, and I can tell that it is quite injured. If it were a person, I would probably say to Hades with any sort of plan and dive down to rescue them. But since it is a wild animal, I think it is best to let nature take its course.

Bel seems satisfied with the thought as well, because he shrugs at me and once again we turn back toward camp. I lose myself in thought as Bellerophon begins his daily routine of exercise and sword practice. While I had made all sorts of battle plans while I was afloat in the void, I had not even thought about taking on a beast. But I quickly come up with a decent plan. Satisfied, I turn to call my companion over and the words dry up in my throat.

He has taken the liberty of removing his tunic while he practices, and his muscles, while not overly defined, ripple with strength. I have never found overly defined muscles to be attractive, even when I was fighting alongside Zeus, Poseidon, and Hades, and all sorts of females were fawning over them, I just did not see what they did. My gaze has lingered far too long, and my face is as hot as a fire, but I can't seem to stop watching. He only has a few hairs on his chest, which is something that I also find appealing, as I don't find overly hairy men attractive either. Fates save me, I think I'm falling for this man, though we've only known each other just over a week.

"I must truly be a sight to behold with how long you've been staring," Bel's voice shakes me out of my stupor. He has a grin on his face, and I so badly wish I could smile back. "That, or you wish you could spar with me."

"Both," the word comes out of my mouth before I can stop it, and I shut my eyes and groan.

His laugh rings out, and I open my eyes to find that he is blushing. "Well, thank you. When you are restored, we will spar as much as you want, Pegasus. Anyway, I've come up with a plan of attack."

"Oh?"

"I think our best bet would be to do a combination of ground and air attacks. Just charge in and catch it off guard."

"Oh, my sweet little Bel… you are good with that sword but you don't have any battle experience, do you?"

CHAPTER ELEVEN

Nike

"Little?" Bellerophon scoffs.

I rolled my eyes. "We cannot just charge in. The chimera is mostly feline, and will have excellent reflexes. We'd be dead before you could get a swing in." Fates grant me patience.

"I didn't think about that... do you have a better plan?"

Raising an eyebrow, I nod. "We have to neutralize its two other heads before we try to take it down. The goat head is the biggest detriment to our stealth. You heard the way it bleats and saw how it's constantly on a swivel. There is no sneaking up on it, so we need to take it out first and foremost. How good a shot are you with a bow?"

"Decent."

"How decent?"

"I can't hit an apple dead in the center off of someone's head, but I can hit a bigger target with precision."

"Perfect. We will start our attack on top of the hill we were scouting on. When the chimera emerges from its cave, you will shoot the goat head."

"Do you suppose it has its own heart?"

"It's hard to say. Your best bet would be right between the eyes, which is a proven kill shot." He nods before pulling his tunic back over his head and I follow him back toward our camp where he starts a fire for dinner.

"Then what?"

"You will hop onto my back and we will dive toward its rear in an attempt to antagonize the snake tail. It's impossible to know if it contains any venom, but it's such an unpredictable part of the beast, and we could easily be pinned down if it gets a hold of one of my legs. I'll get us close and you will lop its head off with your sword before I lift us up higher than the chimera and its fire can reach."

"That makes a lot of sense. So, how do we finish it off?"

I sigh and slump a little. "We need a spear. I didn't even think of asking Hephaestus for one, but then again, I couldn't have known what the monster would look like."

Bel's eyes light up and he jumps to his feet and runs to one of his packs. He rummages around for a moment before returning to the fire with a wrapped package. As he opens it, I can't help the somewhat grin that my mouth breaks into. A beautiful spear head tipped in what appears to be lead sits in his hands. "Uncle H sent this with me, just in case. We just need a shaft for it."

"I can take care of that."

"You don't have any hands, plus… the dryads…" He looks nervous.

"Are you scared of dryads?" I laugh.

"Let's just say one slapped me really hard after I snapped a twig off her tree. I was really young and my father had failed to mention their existence to me."

I can picture a young Bellerophon doing just that, and the thought makes laugh once more. Standing up, I head into the copse of trees until I reach a circle of wildflowers. Lowering myself into an awkward bow as a sign of respect, I call out, "Revered dryads of this land, I come to beseech you for aid!"

The sounds of bodies emerging from trees meets my ears,

but I do not lift my gaze. Dryads are peaceful creatures, for the most part, and they appreciate respect and reverence. It has been a long time since I was in their presence, which used to bring me so much peace after a battle, and I find myself holding back tears for all I've missed out on these few centuries.

"Rise, goddess," a sweet, yet commanding voice greets me.

I lift my head to find that I am surrounded by at least a dozen beautiful young women. One of them stands closer to me than the rest, and I know that it is she who spoke, and who is the leader. She has a deep olive complexion, with dark brown hair studded with dogwood flowers. I attempt a smile, and do my best not to curse the Fates when I remember I'm still a horse.

"My name is Kraneia."

"I am Pegasus."

Her eyes narrow slightly and she gives me an almost unkind smile. "You have come to request our aid, yet you offer a lie in your name?"

Looking around to make sure Bellerophon did not follow me, I sigh, but straighten and meet her gaze. I'd forgotten how perceptive they can be. "My apologies, Kraneia. In this form, which I obtained as part of some sort of curse, I am Pegasus. But in my true form, I am the goddess Nike."

A true, dazzling smile splits all of the dryads' faces. Kraneia bows her head to me. "Welcome, Nike, Goddess of Victory. How may we be of assistance to you? If you are here, you must be doing some sort of fighting, and we are not a warrior people."

"You are correct in that I am here for a fight, but I do not require your help for that. My companion, Bellerophon, and I are here to slay the chimera for King Iobates."

Someone hisses when I say his name, and another snickers. I can only assume that they know the dryad that Bellerophon accidentally slighted when he was young. "We have heard about his plight, as Iobates lives on our lands."

I nod before continuing, "We are in need of a spear shaft so that we may slay the creature. But I dare not take something that does not belong to me. Do you have a piece of wood that we may use?"

Kraneia glances at her companions, who all nod to her. A single tear escapes her eye and a heaviness falls upon our group. "We will give you what you need, because that monster has done so much damage to our forest. It has slaughtered creatures in our care, and it has taken a sister from us," she pauses to scrub the tear from her face before continuing. "You and Morea were kindred spirits in that she had a heart for the vulnerable. That is why you fought in the past, is it not?"

"It is. I lend and will continue to lend my aid to those that need me the most."

She smiles at me. "Morea wasn't a fighter, but she always cared for the animals of our forest, especially the young, ill, and injured. She was trying to protect a small cub from the chimera, and it tore her, limb from limb. Her tree has nearly died with her absence… but her heartwood remains."

With that, Kraneia turns and walks a few steps toward a dying tree. She reaches inside and pulls out a long piece of hardwood that is absolutely beautiful. It is already in the shape of a spear shaft, and about 9 *podes* in length and a *palaiste* in diameter. She held it close and rested her forehead on it for a moment before kissing it and handing it out to me.

"I couldn't," I start, but Kraneia holds up a hand.

"You must. We will bestow Morea's heartwood to you in return for you slaying the beast that slew her. All we ask in return is that you only take the heads needed to satisfy Iobates, and you leave the rest of the chimera's body to us, so we can return it to the earth to nourish our land. And when you are restored to your true body, that this spear remain *your* loyal weapon."

What they are giving me is of the highest of honors, and tears fill my eyes as I nod. "It will be done. I shall call it the Spear of Morea, and I will carry it proudly into battle to defend the vulnerable for the rest of my days. Thank you, Kraneia."

I take the heartwood gingerly into my mouth, and one by one, the dryad come and rest their foreheads to mine in blessing before returning to their trees. "Until we meet again, Nike, and we shall, dear friend," Kraneia embraces me, and then she, too, returns to her tree.

When this is all over, I will return here and thank them once more, and rest from my battles under their care. I take my time walking back to our camp, making sure that I don't damage the wood by whacking it on various trees, since I have to hold it horizontal in my mouth. Oh to have hands again! Reaching camp, I see Bellerophon is just finishing dinner. "That smells good," I say awkwardly around the stick in my mouth.

He looks up and his jaw drops. "Is that heartwood?"

I nod. "Take this please."

His eyes have a look of panic in them, and for a moment, I think he will refuse me, but he shivers and takes it in his hands. "Where did you get this?"

"The dryads gift it to me. It is from the tree of their sister, Morea, whom the chimera slayed. They ask that when this is over, that the spear remain with me, and I have named it after her."

"By all means, you can have it!"

"I think your fear is a little unfounded," I can't help but laugh. He's holding the wood as if it will turn into a serpent and bite him. "It will make the perfect *dory*. Let's connect the spearhead to the shaft."

He does so, then feels the balance. I can tell by the way it sits in his hands that it is perfectly balances, and the two pieces seem like they had always been intended for each other. "Can we practice after we eat?"

We eat quickly, then Bel straps on his armor before putting mine on. He puts his bow and quiver across his back, followed by our near spear, then tightens the sheath with his *xiphos* around his waist. "Ready?"

"I am."

Together, we walk to the middle of the little clearing and I watch as he takes his bow from his back and knocks an arrow. He points to a mound of dirt, indicating that it will be our target. Pulling the bowstring taught, he looses it and the arrow goes through the dirt mound with a thud. Jumping into my saddle, he pulls out his sword as I lift us into the air. Without so much as a soft whinny, that I can't stop to think about how embarrassing it is that I can even make that sound, I dive toward the ground. Bel slashes through the air as I pull up.

We do a few maneuvers, practicing for various scenarios for awhile before he takes the *dory* from his back. I fly around until I'm in a position I like, and sensing it, Bellerophon thrusts the spear into the mound of dirt with a surprising amount of force. I land, and Bel collects his arrow and the spear, then turns to me with a nervous grin. "I say we did pretty good. Let's get some rest. We have a chimera to slay tomorrow."

CHAPTER TWELVE

Bellerophon

My sleep was fitful, and for the past couple of nights, I've been haunted by the same dream. We are flying in the air, and I'm thrown from Pegasus' back. I fall, but before I can reach the ground, I'm caught by a beautiful woman. Well, I can't make out her face, but I can see she has golden hair, and everything about her exudes beauty, grace, and safety. Something about her feels utterly familiar, but I can't place it. She sets me on the ground, and then I realize I can't find Pegasus, and panic overtakes me. That's when I wake up, every time. I hope that it's not a premonition from the Fates that something is going to happen to her, and I'm left the only survivor.

She may be trapped inside a horse's body, but I know that's not who she really is. I so badly want to help her be free of her curse, and I've grown very fond of her. I can't possibly tell her that though, she might think I'm attracted to a horse, but I've started falling for her heart. If she feels the same way, then I hope to have a true relationship with her when she's been restored.

Since I know that sleep will continue to elude me, I open my eyes and find that I'm snuggled up against Pegasus' flank with one of her wings covering me for extra warmth. It makes me smile, and I dare a quick stroke of her soft white feathers before I carefully extricate myself from under her wing. I slip outside our tent quietly and stretch. I've been dreading this day for a couple of weeks now, and while my ever confident companion reassures me everyday that we will be victorious, I find it difficult to see victory in my mind.

May the Fates give Anteia what she deserves for the lies she spun that brought me here. I'm not feeling very hungry, but I know that I'll need my strength for this battle, so I get to work making us a hearty breakfast, even though the sun has barely begun to rise, and Pegasus might not wake up for awhile. I have to do something to keep my mind from coming up with the worse outcomes of this battle. With breakfast cooking, I sit on a large rock and sharpen my *xiphos,* not that it needs sharpening, but it calms my mind with the steady rhythm of whetstone against metal.

"You're up early," Pegasus' quiet, yet always confident, voice breaks the stillness.

"Couldn't sleep," I mutter. "I figured I could get a head start on breakfast and sharpen my blade before you woke up. Why are you up so early?"

"I *always* wake up early before a battle," she says as if she's seen many. And maybe she has, but she hasn't shared much about her past with me. There is so much fear hidden behind her bright blue eyes, but not for the fight ahead of it. No, it's fear of her true identity coming to light. I wish she would just tell me what makes her so afraid so I can protect her.

"And what do you do with your time?" I ask instead of prying, even though I really want to.

"Stretch, meditate on my battle plans, and eat well. It does no good to go into battle with an empty stomach. What I wouldn't give for a little ambrosia."

"I wonder…" I start, cutting myself off as I sheath my

sword and stand. "My father supplied me with an extra pack of rations, and I noticed a small bottle in there, but I've yet to open it."

Reaching my pack with Pegasus close behind me, I rummage around until my fingers grasp onto the vial. I pull it out and uncork it, a sweet intoxicating smell escapes from inside as I do so. "By the Fates!" She exclaims, taking a big whiff. "Could you pour that into our porridge?"

"I will! I can't believe Poseidon actually gave me some of his ambrosia. He's quite greedy when it comes to his sweets," I explain as I mix it into the porridge, which has just finished cooking.

We slip into a comfortable silence as we eat and watch the sun rise, the various shades of pink and purple illuminating the sky in a sort of promise of good things to come. Not wanting to stall any longer, I rise and walk over to my armor, and start to methodically put it on piece by piece. I look up from grabbing one of my bracers to find Pegasus watching me very intently, her white hair slightly pink. I can't help but flex and wiggle my eyebrows at her. She shakes her head with a giggle, the sound of which gives me butterflies.

"Hurry up water boy, I can't put my armor on myself."

I grin at her and slowly finish putting my armor arm. She rolls her eyes in disbelief before grabbing my helmet off the ground with her mouth and prancing away. "Hey! Bring that back!"

"You can have it once my armor is in place," she replies after stashing it in the tent.

"Fine," I sigh as I tighten the laces of my boots.

I put each piece of her armor on with care, making sure they're all cinched tightly and have no chance of coming off. It worries me, though, because there are still so many unarmored spots of her body, so many weak spots. I have to make sure she doesn't get hurt. "All done. How does it feel?"

She trots around our camp to get a feel for the sturdiness of the armor before nodding at me, "You did well. Thank you." Then she retrieves my helmet and hands it out to me, and I promptly put it on my head. She groans, much to my confusion and then delight. "How can you make *armor* look attractive?"

"What can I say, I enhance the beauty of everything that touches me."

Pegasus snorts, then leans her head against mine, much like my favorite horse back home does. "Trust the plan, trust your instincts, and trust *me*. I won't let you be harmed, Bel. We will walk away from this victorious."

I swallow a lump in my throat and nod, unable to speak, and I softly brush her neck for a moment. No more time for dallying, it's time to slay the chimera before it has a chance to wreak anymore havoc.

We crest the top of the hill, moving very slowly so our gear makes no noise. Peaking over, I can see that the beast has yet to emerge from its cave, though I can hear it rustling around. I steady my shaking hands as I reach behind me and grab the bow from my back. Pegasus uses her mouth to pluck an arrow out of my quiver and offers it to me. I knock it, and then we wait. And wait. And wait some more.

I'm about to lower myself to the ground to sit when the lion-headed beast finally emerges from the cave, spewing some fire as it approaches what remains of the wild boar it caught yesterday. Pegasus levels her gaze on me and nods, changing her stance so that she's ready to launch into the air after I complete phase one of our battle plan.

I take a few deep breaths as I raise my weapon and pull the bowstring taught. The goat head, thankfully, can't see us, and I take one more steadying breath as I aim for the spot right between its eyes. My fingers let loose and the arrow makes impact exactly where I was aiming, and the goat head lolls limply to the side. The lion head, however, roars as I jump up into the saddle and Pegasus launches us airborne.

I unsheathed my *xiphos* with one hand and grip the reins tightly with the other so I don't fall off as she does somewhat of a nose dive. She swoops down with a battle cry, and the snake headed tail of the chimera bolts up. Its mouth opens, revealing large fangs as it hisses and raises itself to snap at her legs. Letting go of the reins, I use both hands to cut downward with as much force as possible, and I feel my blade meet resistance as it slices through the snake. I watch as the head falls to the ground, the rest of the trail dropping.

The chimera roars violently as it whirls around, a clawed paw narrowly missing Pegasus' underbelly as her wings beat down, lifting us higher. She dodges the stream of flames aimed for her. "Bellerophon!" She yells over the chimera's roar. "Get the spear! You're going to have to jab at it until just the right moment for it to open its jaws. That's when you'll sink it down its throat for the kill shot."

I don't bother answering with my voice, but I squeeze my legs around her sides twice so she knows I heard her. Sheathing my sword, I draw the *dory* from my back, and it seems to hum in anticipation. The way Pegasus moves through the air is like an elegant dance as we antagonize the chimera, trying to force it in just the right position. She dodges every flame and I get several jabs in. We move in this dance far longer than I thought we would have to fight, but I grit my teeth and keep going.

Pegasus suddenly banks right and drops down. We're too low. The chimera is stretching out its claws and I watch in horror as they meet her flesh. "Now Bellerophon!" She roars in pain as the chimera opens its mouth to throw flames her way. Without hesitation, I hurl the spear as hard as I can down its throat. It keels around, its legs wobbling beneath it, and then collapses.

With a gasp of pain, Pegasus lands beside it and I immediately dismount, bending down to check her wound. "I'm fine!" She snaps, though I know she's not trying to be rude. "You need to behead the monster quickly, just in case."

I don't want to do anything but tend to her, but she's right. There will be time for me to assess her wounds later. Grabbing the three waterproof leather sacks from the only saddle bag I attached for the fight, I stalk to the body of the monster and wrench the spear from its maws. Then I draw my *xiphos* and in a swift motion, I remove the lion head. I place it in one of the sacks, then walk around it to pick up the snake head, which goes in a second sack. I have to climb on top of the carcass to reach the goat head, and its body heat radiates off of it as I ascend. It takes only one more strike with my sword to remove the goat head, and I place it into the last sack.

When I reach Pegasus, her heavy breathing has stopped and she looks at me with pride. "Well done. I told you we'd be victorious."

"Thank you. I'm sorry you were hurt," I say, bending to check her wound once more.

"Not here. Let's go back to camp."

"Are you ok to fly?"

"It's nothing but a scratch," she attempts to wave me off with one of her hooves. "Please, Bel."

Gritting my teeth so I don't say anything rude, I quickly tie the sacks to her saddle and hop astride. Muttering about the extra weight, which, to be fair, is quite a bit, Pegasus extends her wings and flaps them down, gently lifting us up. We soar over the hill and make it back to camp much quicker than we would have gotten there by walking.

As soon as we land, I start tearing off her armor, throwing each piece to the side. In frustration at my limited view, I grab my helmet and fling it away from me. "Pegasus. You're bleeding pretty badly," I say as I finally take in the five jagged claw marks along her belly. "They look fairly deep."

"I'm fine, you finish taking off your armor."

CHAPTER THIRTEEN

Nike

"You are *not* fine!" Bellerophon bellows. "You are going to need stitches. I don't think I even have enough thread for how many gashes you have."

His face has paled, and he's shaking as he tries to remove his armor. It is not going well, and I can't help the small giggle that escapes me as I watch him. Just earlier I couldn't take my eyes off of him as he expertly put his gear on. For some reason it was one of the most attractive things I've ever seen. And now, he looks extremely clumsy as he's flinging each piece in various directions, and this sight is nearly as attractive to me. Has Eros shot me with one of his love arrows? This is ridiculous.

While my wound is painful and indeed bleeding, I don't think it calls for his level of panic. I'm a goddess, I'll heal eventually. I'm more worried about the pain I'm going to feel when he attempts to stitch me up. "Do you have any experience with stitching?" I ask. I could do it myself if I didn't have hooves, I've had to do it before.

"Believe it or not, yes. I've gotten myself into trouble here and there growing up," he replies as he finally removes his last piece of armor. I watch as he grab his needle and and golden thread from one of the saddle bags. "This is going to hurt." His voice is calm, but I can see the concern in his eyes.

"I know."

"The last thing I want to do is hurt you," he whispers, reaching a hand up to caress my neck.

My body shudders a little at his touch, and he puts his forehead against mine. "I'll be alright, Bel."

Letting out a breath, he nods and beckons for me to lay down. I do so, rolling more onto my side so that my belly is exposed. If I were in my normal body as a woman, this would be entirely inappropriate, but I try not to think about it too much as I brace myself for the pain. Bellerophon meets my eyes, asking for permission to begin without using any words. I give him what I hope resembles an encouraging smile, and then I feel the needle pierce my skin.

I grit my teeth and blink rapidly; I refuse to cry. It takes him quite a while to stitch up all five claw marks, but I'm relieved to see that he still has thread on his spool as he ties off the last stitch. My belly burns, but I'm thankful to no longer be bleeding. "Thank you, Bel."

"You're welcome, Pegasus. I wish there was more I could do. What I wouldn't give for some salve."

"We can help with that," a voice interjects.

Bellerophon flinches and seems to restrain himself from making himself seem smaller as he catches sight of who the voice belongs to. I roll my eyes and look over my shoulder, my gaze meeting Kraneia's. "We did it, Kraneia. The chimera is dead."

"I know, Pegasus. We returned its body to the land. And since you kept your promise, my sisters and I came to see if you required our assistance. It looks like you do," the dryad said, producing a small jar from her satchel. "This is a healing salve, and it offers a cooling sensation for your burning skin."

Tears of gratitude fill my eyes as she bends down and

applies the salve. I bite back a laugh as I watch the other women shoo Bellerophon away and begin to prepare our midday meal. The instant relief I feel as the salve cools my wounds is enough to let one of the tears escape my eye. "Thank you, Kraneia."

"And thank you, my friend. Already the forest seems brighter."

We dine together as a group, and it makes me happy to see the tension melt away from Bellerophon's shoulders as he converses with the dryads. They seem to have forgiven him his slight as a youth. Kraneia leaves the jar of salve with Bel, and instructs him to apply it three times a day until the stitches come out, though I hope that I can apply it myself before then. The thought makes my body slump, though. Why am I still trapped in this body?"

"Pegasus?" I look up to see Bel looking at me with concern. I haven't spoken in quite some time, not since the dryads left nearly an hour ago. "What's wrong?"

"We slayed the chimera, fulfilling the quest… so why am I still a winged horse? I think I showed courage with our fight, especially by putting myself in a vulnerable position and allowing myself to be wounded so you could get the perfect shot."

He scrunches his eyebrows and runs a hand through his scruffy facial hair that he hasn't bothered shaving the entire journey. "Perhaps you will be returned to your proper form after we deliver the heads to King Iobates. Technically we haven't completed the quest until we do so."

"I suppose you're right. Well, what are we waiting for? Let's go to his palace," I try to stand, but my legs wobble and I end up back on the ground.

Bel raises an eyebrow. "You were wounded three hours ago. Your body needs time to rest. We will see if you are well enough tomorrow. For now, try to get some sleep. I need to retrieve our armor and get everything sorted and packed up. I'll wake you when I have dinner ready."

Knowing there's no point in arguing, I nod and close my eyes. As I'm drifting off, I feel a blanket cover my body, and I fall asleep with a hint of a smile on my face.

CHAPTER FOURTEEN

Bellerophon

After covering Pegasus with the blanket, I watch as she drifts off to sleep. When I can see that her breathing is even and steady, I turn away, running a hand through my hair. Her wounds had scared me pretty badly, worse than actually fighting the chimera itself. They were much deeper than I let on, and I was terrified that I wouldn't be able to close them well enough. Thank the Fates that I had enough thread, and another thanks to my father for providing it. The salve from the dryads seems to be working wonders for her as well, and for that I am eternally grateful to them.

As much as I'm looking forward to this quest being complete, a part of me is dreading seeing Iobates. The spiteful man with his hateful daughter, not even asking for my side of the story before asking for my life. I'd like to teach him a thing or two with my fists. But no, that wouldn't do. If he tries to demand more from me, I may challenge him to a duel. There's no way the old man can still fight as he could in his youth.

I can feel myself getting riled up, so I take a deep breath and focus on the steady rising and falling of Pegasus's body as she sleeps, her breathing comforting me. Tomorrow, if she is well enough, we will deliver the chimera's heads to King Iobates and her form will be restored. I find that I can't wait to meet her, the *real* her. And even if there is more that we have to do in order to free her from her curse, I will remain by her side for as long as she'll have me. Feeling resolve, I straighten up our camp, repacking the saddle bags and packs. I make sure the chimera's heads are secure in their sacks and aren't leaking through. Thankfully the mess is still contained inside.

When I am satisfied with the state of our camp, I head into the tent for a quick nap. I awake only an hour later, but I feel fairly rested. Pegasus is still sleeping, which means her body is healing, and for that, I am grateful. My stomach rumbles, so I suppose that now is as good a time as any to start preparing dinner. I hate to wake her when it's done cooking, but she needs sustenance in order to heal properly.

"Pegasus," I call out to her, gently shaking one of her shoulders.

"Hmm?" She asks sleepily.

I smile and stroke her mane. "Dinner is ready. You need to eat, and I need to apply the salve again."

She groans but rolls away from me, exposing her belly. I'm surprised to see that the redness has already gone down tremendously, and while is still more hot to the touch than it should be, the wound looks much better. Perks of being a goddess, I suppose. I gently apply the salve as she wakes up fully.

"How does it look?"

"It actually looks a lot better. How are you feeling?"

"I feel like I got punched by a titan, if I'm being honest. A nice hot meal should help though."

"Punched by a titan?" I laugh.

"It's quite painful, actually," she replies very seriously.

"Wait, you've actually encountered titans? They've been

gone for centuries."

"And I've been stuck in a void for those centuries. Bel, I fought in the war against the titans."

We've kind of talked about her past, but she never really gives much detail. I should have known that those wars are where her experience comes from, yet it's still hard to wrap my head around it. "So, are you actually an old hag?" I tease, not knowing what else to say.

She stands, the movement slow, and pain flashes across her face before it is replaced with an incredulous look. "I'll have you know that I am actually a young woman, thank you very much."

"A beautiful young woman?"

"Yes. I mean, I may not be the most beautiful, but I've been told I'm quite lovely."

She's blushing, and I can't help but chuckle. We eat our dinner, then retire to our tent. It make my heart skip a beat when she raises one of her wings for me, so without a word, I lay beside her and allow her warm, soft, feathery wing to blanket over me. Tomorrow, we will complete this quest.

The morning comes too quickly for my liking, but Pegasus is up before I am, impatiently waiting to head out. It doesn't bother me though, I know I would want to break a curse quickly if I were under one. Though, I suppose, I did want to get this quest over with quickly so I could get on with my life. We eat some figs and honey as a light meal, I apply some more salve to her wounds, and then I place her saddle on back.

"Please make sure those sacks aren't leaking. I really don't want my hair stained any redder than it already is from my wounds," Pegasus instructs with a grown.

"Don't worry, they haven't leaked at all," I say, holding one up to show her.

The heads are heavier than one would expect, and I feel bad for adding so much extra weight to her load as I tie each one carefully to her saddlebags. She grunts as I finally swing myself up, our camp completely cleared. The only evidence that anyone was ever here is a dead fireplace. I know our dryad friends will approve of our cleanliness.

It takes her a little more effort to carry us into the sky than normal, but she she steadies out as her wings take on the full load of all the weight. Since we are technically in Iobates' territory, it only takes an hour or so before his palace comes into view. I use the reins to gently guide her in the direction of the courtyard, where she lands far more gracefully than I expected her to, due to her wounds and the weight she's carrying.

Several guards run up to us, hands on their weapons. "Peace, men. I am Bellerophon, son of Poseidon, and I'm here to deliver the bounty that King Iobates asked for."

They look at me with skepticism, so I untie the sacks and hold one open for them to inspect. Their faces turn a little green and one rushes inside the palace, probably to let the king know we've arrived. When he returns, he beckons us to follow. Pegasus steps with me, and one of the guard holds up a hand.

"No animals in the palace."

"Excuse me?" Pegasus narrows her eyes at the guard, a lethal edge in her voice. The man's eyes widen in surprise.

"She's not an animal, you *malakas*," I shake my head. "This is Pegasus, a goddess trapped in a from that isn't hers. And she will go where she pleases, are we clear?"

Smartly, the man nods and ushers us to go ahead. We are led to the throne room, where the semi-rotund king lounges on his overly embellished throne. His gray hair is offset by the golden crown resting on top of his head, and he is dressed in his very best, it seems. There is a ring on each of his large fingers, in a display of his sloth and wealth it seems.

"Presenting Bellerophon, son of Poseidon, and his companion, the goddess Pegasus!" Someone bellows as we enter the room.

Without waiting for him to call us closer, I stalk toward Iobates, the three sacks swinging in my grasp as I walk. When I'm just a couple steps away, I fling the sacks down, the heads spilling out and rolling toward him. All three of them end up facing him, and their mouths are open, it's truly a horrendous sight. The man squeals and hops up to where he's standing on his throne. Pathetic. "All *three* heads of the chimera, King Iobates. You only requested one, so you could say that I've over delivered. So the bounty for my life shall be removed."

He looks like he wants to chastise me for making a demand of him, a *king*, but he seems to remember that I'm technically a Demi-god. "Citizens!" He yells out to all who are gathered in the throne room. "Please welcome our hero, Bellerophon, who has slain the legendary chimera terrorizing our kingdom!"

The room breaks out in a loud applause, which I was not

expecting. Pegasus waggles her eyebrows at me, and though it might be childish, I stick my tongue out at her. "You have done this kingdom a great service, and have redeemed yourself, son."

"He is not your son," Pegasus says before I can. "And you will do well to respect his status, Iobates."

The courage of this woman is like no other, to openly address a king, albeit a mortal one, without his title in front of his subject. I love it. Perhaps this is the courage she needed to be restored. But nothing happens as I watch her, and my heart sinks a little.

"Indeed," he scoffs a little.

"And the next time you jump straight to calling for someone's execution based on what your daughter says, you should do a little more investigating and check both sides of the story," I put in. "Your precious daughter is a liar. I *never* tried to kiss her. She's the one who cornered *me*."

"That's an outrageous accusation," he says between gritted teeth.

Pegasus shakes her head and glares at the man. He shrinks back a little, for although she is a horse, she's thrice his size and radiates power. He clears his throat and spreads his arms out in a welcoming gesture. "To show our gratitude for all you've done for us, we will have a celebratory feast in your honor!" The crowd roars with delight, but I can't help but groan.

My companion, on the other hand, looks very pleased. "What, I like excellent food, alright?" She attempts a shrug. "We should be rewarded as such."

And then, we are separated. I'm taken to a very nice room and told to bathe. "My companion?" I ask a servant.

"She's down the hall, sir. We will make sure she is cleaned up and ready for supper," the man assures me.

Satisfied, I do as I'm told and bathe. It feels good to take a hot bath after rinsing off in cold streams for our entire journey. After my bath, I climb up into the luxurious bed and drift off for a nap. My last thought before I'm out is that I hope Pegasus has them apply her salve.

CHAPTER FIFTEEN

Nike

Never in my life have I felt more violated and vulnerable than I did having those servants wash me down in this palace chamber. They basically created a makeshift stall in this room, and placed the mattress on the floor for me to lie down on. I will say that I no longer smell like an animal and my mane has been combed and braided in a very beautiful manner. What I wouldn't give for a soft pelops to wear, but that would so look very unbecoming in my current state.

After a decent nap, I've been pacing my room waiting for someone to fetch me. I don't like to be confined in an unfamiliar place, and I have no means of escape should something go wrong. The window is much too small for my horse body to fit through and the only way for me to open the door is to knock it down. Finally, there is a knock at my door, and I'm pleased to see Bellerophon stepping in. "We have been summed for the feast," he says.

"Finally! I'm starving," I say as I follow him and a servant down the hall. "You clean up nicely. And you have a handsome face under that scruff!"

He laughs, running a hand over his freshly shaved jaw. "Figured I should attempt to look my best since this is a feast in our honor."

The dining hall is absolutely packed, and the delicious smells of food flood the entire room. My mouth waters as we are led to our seats. Bel is seated to the right of the king, and I'm seating to Bel's right. They cleared a large spot for me, and I'm grateful, but I can't help but feel embarrassed that I can't use a chair and eat properly. Iobates gives a speech and toast, and then everyone digs in. It is by far the best meal I have ever eaten.

When we finally return to our sleeping quarters, I nudge Bellerophon's shoulder. "It didn't work, Bel. I'm still a horse."

"I know," he sighs, giving me a sympathetic look.

"I think there's only one thing left for me to do," and at his questioning look, I continue, "Maybe someone on Olympus can help me. I've been hiding from Zeus because I don't know if he can be trusted. It's the reason my parents banished me to the void to begin with. But I may have to face him for help. Will you go with me tomorrow?"

"Pegasus, I will go anywhere with you, even to Tartarus if you ask me."

That makes me smile. "Olympus it is. It should only take us a few hours of flying to get there. We will leave first thing in the morning."

Iobates bids us farewell in his courtyard, asking that should he need our aid, if he could send for us. He may be a frustrating old man that jump to conclusions, but if his people are in danger, I am happy to return and help them. Bellerophon begrudgingly agreed. And then we were off. Olympus can be seen for miles around, so all I have to do is fly toward it. The closer we get, however, the tighter his legs squeeze my flanks.

"What's wrong, water boy?"

"I have a bad feeling about this. I may not be entirely mortal, but I know for a fact the gods don't take lightly to people showing up on Olympus without an invitation. My father may be one of the gods of the pantheon, but that doesn't give me the right barge up there."

"It will be alright. I promise I won't let anything happen to you. Besides, Zeus owes me big time."

"Don't make a promise you can't keep, Pegasus. I may have been having dreams during our journey, that seem more like premonitions. And the feeling in my gut tells me that it's about to come true."

We've reached the mountain Olympus sits upon, and I begin ascending toward its peak. "It's going to be alright, just hold on tight—" I'm cut off by a booming voice as my wings lift us ever higher.

"Who dares to approach the home of the gods!" That voice can only belong to Zeus.

I don't bother answering. I'm too winded, and he can ask all the questions he wants once I reach the top.

"Halt your approach now, or face my wrath!"

I roll my eyes. So dramatic. At least that hasn't changed. The city is coming into view now, and I can see the man who was once my friend standing in the courtyard of his palace, a large lighting bolt pointed down toward us. And then it's hurtling toward us.

"Father no!" Artemis screams as she launches herself toward her father.

In a panic, I pull my wings tight against my back to drop down quickly, but I'm not quick enough. A strangled neigh escapes my throat as the lightening bolt hits me square in the chest, and I rear up. I didn't even have time to tell my companion to hold on. And then, a weight disappears from my back, and I look down to see Bellerophon falling toward the ground, his eyes wide with panic and fear.

"No! Bellerophon!" I scream.

Angling myself down I try to dive through the air to get to him, but he's falling faster than I can drop, and even if I could get to him, I don't know how I could catch him. "Pegasus!" He cries, and my heart shatters.

"Help me!" I bellow, my voice echoing off of Olympus.

Time seems to stand still as a golden light rushes toward me, and then I'm enveloped in it. My body feels lighter, and I pull up, bringing my hands to my face. Wait. My *hands*! I look down to see that I am a woman once more, and without a second hesitation, I dive for all I'm worth toward the ground.

The ground is coming up fast and I stretch a hand out. Bellerophon's eyes are nearly popping out of his head as he reaches one arm up toward me. Make it, make it, make it, I repeat to myself. He's just a handful of *podes* away from his death, and I stretch my arm as far as I can. His hand grasps mine, and with a cry of relief and victory, I yank him up and press him firmly against my body. Our breathing is quite labored as I right myself and begin the assent once more.

Wriggling in my grasp, I loosen my hold on him so he can look at me. "It's you," he gasps. "The woman from my dream, the one that saved me every time. I know you."

"Of course you know me, water boy. We've been traveling together for weeks now." Did the fall go to his head or something?

He rolls his eyes and shakes his head. "I mean, I've seen you before. Well, your statues, at least."

"Statues?"

"Yeah, Zeus and Athena had several commissioned in your honor after Kronos was successfully defeated… after you disappeared. You're Nike!"

My smile lights up my entire face, and he blushes brightly at the slight. "The Goddess of Victory at your service," I bow my head at him.

"How did I not figure it out sooner?"

"I mean, I *was* a horse. But I did drop some hints."

"Are you really still taking us up there?"

"Of course I am. Zeus nearly killed the man of my dreams and he is going to answer for that," I tell him matter of factly.

He stares at me in astonishment as I land on the opposite side of the courtyard to where a crowd has gathered. I set him on his own two feet and turn to go give Zeus a piece of my mind, but Bellerophon catches my hand and pulls me toward him. And before I can get a word out, his arms are around me and his lips are on mine. It's a sweet kiss, full of unspoken words and promises, and my entire body heats up as I melt into him for too short of a moment.

With a sheepish look, he releases me. "I never imagined that the woman of my dreams would rescue me or be able to carry me as if I weigh nothing. And while part of my feels like I should be embarrassed about that, I think it makes me even more attracted to you."

I laugh and give him a bright smile. "We shall resume this later, that I can assure you."

Then I turn once more and lock eyes with the man who was once my friend, and who has turned incredibly pale. "N-Nike? Is that really you?"

It gives me great joy to see both Artemis and Athena glaring daggers at him. There is a weight on my back, and I reach behind me to feel the Spear of Morea strapped there. I don't know how that happened, but I grin as I pull it from my back and point it at Zeus' throat. His eyes widen and he gulps. This man has gotten too big of a head while I've been gone, and he needs to be brought down a few steps. "Zeus. Care to explain why you tried to kill me and the man I love?"

"Love?" I hear Bellerophon repeat from behind me, but I don't have the time to explain what I realized as I watched him nearly plummet to his death.

"I didn't know it was you," Zeus explains as he puts his hands up in surrender.

I push the tip of the spear into his neck a little harder before I remove it and place it behind my back once more. "No, you didn't. But you decided that you get to take the life of any living thing that flies too close to home? That's not the man I helped to defeat the titans. Where has this ego come from?"

"You tell him, Nike!" Artemis pumps her fist in the air, and I have to work extraordinarily hard not to smile in response.

"You're right, my friend. I guess I got a little to full of myself being the king of the gods. Forgive me, please."

"Apologize to your nephew, too."

Zeus' eyes widen even further as he finally takes in my companion.

"Bellerophon?"

"Uncle," his voice is flat.

"Forgive me for trying to kill you. I didn't know. You are always welcome here, both of you."

I roll my eyes but nod at him. "Forgiven, for now. But you owe me, my old friend, and I would like to collect."

"Of course, anything. But first, where have you been all these years?"

"We sent her to a place outside of space and time," a familiar, feminine voice meets me ears and my eyes well up with tears as I whirl around to see my mother. She has appeared behind me, along with my father.

Without thinking, I run toward them and fling myself into their arms. All three of us are sobbing, but I don't care. I've waited so long to be reunited with my parents. "We didn't mean to send you away for so long," my father says quietly.

"When we tried to call you back, we realized that we had mixed up one of our words, and we couldn't bring you back. We knew that something would bring you back to us, it was just a matter of waiting," Styx continued.

"Word got back to us that a magnificent winged horse had sprung from the head of a gorgon, and we just knew that it was you, but your mother and I had no idea where you had gone, so we decided to wait here, knowing you'd show up eventually," Pallas finished.

I turned back to Zeus, who was listening intently to everything. "But why did you send her away in the first place?"

"We had heard rumors that you may have wanted to use her to assert your rule over the rest of the gods, and we would not have that," my mother crossed her arms.

"What? I would never have done that. It must have been a last ditch effort of Kronos to sow discord among us. I'm so sorry that you thought I'd do that to my best friend."

I shrug, "What's done is done."

"So, where have you been since you returned?" He asked, leading us inside his palace and gesturing that we should all sit and get comfortable.

"Do you want to tell him, or should I?" I ask Bellerophon as he sits beside me. He's still looking at me with awe, and maybe adoration as well.

"You can tell them what you were doing until we met," he says before stealing another quick kiss.

"Fair enough. I floated in a dark abyss for centuries I

suppose, though I couldn't tell how time was passing. Then suddenly I was pulled from the void and found myself in a cave looking at a young man whose name was Perseus."

At the mention of that name, Zeus perked up with a grin. "That's one of my sons!"

"So he told me. Anyway, I apparently just sprang out of the gorgon Medusa's head, and then I flew until I found a safe looking forest, and woke up the next morning in Artemis' presence. She gave me a place to stay until Athena came and asked me to help Bel."

I turn to my companion, the man I have fallen for, and nod for him to continue the story.

CHAPTER SIXTEEN

Bellerophon

"King Iobates of Lycia sent a missive to my father asking for my head because his daughter claimed that I had tried to kiss her. She's a married woman, and in his kingdom, that is grounds for execution. She is the one that tried to kiss me, and I declined because of the fact that she is married, but apparently out of spite, she ran to her father and lied about the whole thing."

It still fills me with rage that she did that. But if she hadn't, I never would have met Pegasus, I mean, Nike. I can't believe I've been with the Goddess of Victory this whole time, that I've fallen in love with her, even though I didn't know who she truly was. And she seems to feel the same way about me.

"He told my father that he would take the head of the chimera, which had been terrorizing his kingdom instead of my head. So I was sent on a quest to slay the beast. I asked for a companion to accompany me, and Aunt Athena said she would ask Artemis for help. They asked Pegasus, a winged horse, to accompany and she said yes. I had no idea she was really Nike."

Zeus seems very intrigued by our story, and I do my best to not give any sort of indication that I see my father has appeared behind his brother. He seems quite put out and has a mischievous look in his eyes, and I don't want to interrupt whatever scheme he has going. Instead, I wink at Nike before continuing.

"We made the journey, first stopping to see Hephaestus for some armor for her. Speaking of which, where did all of our gear go?"

"I grabbed it with my chariot after she was hit and you fell," a man says. I look up to see Apollo waving at me.

"Thank you." He nods. "We traveled to the chimera's lair, and with Nike's expertise, came up with a plan of attack after scouting the creature and its habits for a day. The beast was slain, we delivered the heads to Iobates, but she was still Pegasus. She was told that she had to complete the quest and learn true courage to be restored. She showed so much courage, but the curse hadn't been broken. Which led us here, and you know the rest."

As soon as the last word leaves my mouth, Poseidon opens his hands over Zeus and a stream of seawater pours over top of his head, complete with seaweed and a couple small fish. Everyone erupts with laughter, except for Zeus, who tackle my father. It's comical to watch them wrestle, and eventually they both get up laughing. "That was for trying to kill my son. It would have been a lot worse had you actually succeeded."

"Dually noted."

Artemis snaps her fingers and stands up. "I got it! Nike, the courage you needed to find was facing the unknown with my father, and then you abandoned it in order to save Bellerophon!"

It made sense to me, and I'm sure she's thinking the same thing. I feel a tap on my shoulder and see Nike beckoning me to follow her. "Bel, can we talk?" She leads us to a secluded corner and sits on a stone bench.

"Everything alright?" I ask, cause she looks more nervous than I've ever seen her.

"I'm going to ask something quite big of Zeus, but before I do, I'd like to know where we stand."

"Where we stand?"

"Well, you heard me admit my feelings, quite unceremoniously, I'm afraid."

She blushes a deep crimson, and it makes her golden hair stand out. I always imagined her hair would be blonde, and she still has the same blue eyes. "I fell in love with the woman inside of the horse quite some time ago."

Her answering smile makes my heart skip a beat again, and I feel a little bit like a lovesick fool. She takes my large, rough hand in hers, and it surprises me that her skin is so soft, since she is a warrior of the highest order. "This is going to be quite uncustomary, but would you perhaps want to marry me?" She asks, and I can feel my eyes bug out of my head.

"You mean to tell me, that *thee* Goddess of Victory, wants to marry a measly demigod? You're not even going to court me first?"

Nike rolls her eyes, but she doesn't try to hide her grin. "Indeed. We will have time for courting later. But I'm afraid without marriage involved, Zeus may deny my request."

"I'd be a fool to say no, and I may be a lot of things, but Fates now I'm no fool. And I will court you properly, that I promise you." I squeeze her hand. "What are you going to ask him to do?"

"It's better you are unaware at the moment. Just... trust me, alright?"

Then she takes a deep breath, picks herself up to her full height, and walks toward Zeus' throne.

CHAPTER SEVENTEEN

Nike

Never in a millennia would I ever have imagined I would ask a man to marry me. But here we are. Everyone seems to be able to tell that I have business to attend to, and the room grows quiet. I flash a reassuring smile at my parents, and my father winks at me. I have been confident for as long as I can remember, but I can feel may resolve waver a fraction, just for a moment. What if Zeus says no?

"I assume it's time I gave you what you're due. Ask me, my friend. I will grant you any request. You were the reason we were ultimately victorious against the titans, and I never got to thank you properly for that. And after the incident this afternoon… I owe you a lot."

"All I ask is that you grant Bellerophon the gift of immortality, and that you wed us before all of these witnesses. He is the only man that I have ever loved, and he loves the people of this land as much as I do. I cannot imagine going into battle without him by my side, and without that gift, he will only be with me for so many fights."

There are some murmurs in the room, and for the first time, I get a glimpse of Hera. I always knew those two were destined for each other, and even now, after everything I heard that Zeus has done by not being faithful to her, there is still so much love for him in her eyes. Without a word, she walks up to her husband and places a hand on his arm, and when he turns to her, she places the other on his face. The look she gives him is so lovey dovy, that I almost cringe, but I know that I will always look at Bellerophon that way. She nods at him, and he closes his eyes and leans into her touch for a moment before straightening and meeting my gaze once more.

"It shall be done."

The room breaks out in applause, and I gesture for Bellerophon to stand by my side. He looks to be in shock, but he grins broadly at me anyway. "You want me to be immortal?" He whispers into my ear.

"I don't think I can live my immortal life without you," I say as he kisses my cheek.

From her pocket, Hera produces a small vial, and Zeus shoots a small lightening bolt into it. The vial glows, and he holds it out for Bellerophon to take. "Drink this, it's a mixture of Ambrosia, a secret ingredient, and my power. And it will grant you godhood."

Bel pulls the cork out, and with nervous look toward me, downs the mixture in one gulp. A golden glow emanates from his body, and as it dissipates, there is a very subtle change to him. His features seem just a bit sharper, and I can see the hint of an aura around him. In time, he will learn to control how much of it is visible. I smile at him, relief washing over me. The man of my dreams will not grow old and die. He will live through eternity with me.

"Thank you," Bellerophon says to both Zeus and me.

"Now, I suppose it's time for a wedding!" Zeus exclaims.

My mother comes up to my side and offers me a veil. Where she got it from, I don't know, but I bow my head and let her place sit in my hair. The fabric of the veil is attached to a circlet made of gold laurel leaves, the symbol of victory. *My* symbol.

"Do you, Bellerophon, take Nike to be your wife, now and for all the ages?"

"I do."

"And Nike, do you take Bellerophon to be your husband, now and for all the ages."

"I do."

Hera bumps Zeus to the side with her hip. "And as the goddess of marriage, I bless this union. May it forever be full of love, laughter, and victorious battles."

"Yeah, what she said," Zeus chuckles.

Bellerophon takes me in his arms, and I draw my wings tightly against my back as he dips me, kissing me softly. I know that he will make good on his promise to court me, that this marriage will be built on more than what we already have, and I look forward to our future together. The applause in the room dies down, and someone clears their throat.

A younger god, who looks like a mortal teenager, hovers above us with winged shoes. His cheeks are a deep crimson, and I know he did not relish the fact that he interrupted our wedding. "H-hi," he gives me an awkward little wave and then clears his throat. "The name is Hermes, messenger god. I'm sorry to cut in on this important event, but I have an urgent message from King Iobates of Lycia."

Bel groans and I gently elbow him in the stomach. "And what, by all the Fates, could he possibly want? We just saw him this morning."

Hermes rubbed the back of his neck and sighed. "He says that a tribe of Amazons, legendary warrior women, have invaded the far reaches of his territory and are slaughtering whole villages. The king asked that I emphasize that he is begging for your help in saving his people."

The thought of innocent women and children being

slaughtered by these so-called Amazons makes my stomach boil. A hand taps my shoulder, and I turn to see my father holding my *xiphos,* the one I had fought with so many years ago. It still looks as though it's new. I grin at him as I strap the belt around my waist as my mother hands me my old armor. My new husband doesn't miss a beat, and heads over to where Apollo is holding his armor out to him.

Once we are both fully clad in our armor, I turn to my husband and grin at him. "Well, husband, what do you say about honeymooning on a battle field?"

"Where you go, I go, Nike. I will follow you into every battle."

"I know this is supposed to be the man's job, so you'll have to forgive me," I laugh as I scoop him up in my arms. "But we are in a hurry."

Turning to my family and friend, I lift a hand in farewell, and launch us into the air, heading toward the thing I was made to do: bring victory in battle.

CHAPTER EIGHTEEN

Epilogue-Bellerophon

I awaken in the early morning hours and gently extricate my arm from under my sleeping wife. It's been a month, and I still can't believe that this beautiful, confident, amazing goddess is my Fates blessed *wife*; it feels like a dream. We battled the Amazon women for a solid two weeks. They were a challenging tribe, but Nike was able to push them back into their own territory, and instead of slaughtering them all, brokered peace with them. I am still amazed at that. She told me that victory is more than just killing all of your enemies. Sometimes victory lies in bringing peace, and that's exactly what she did.

Her pelops is crumpled and wrinkled, and there are still some blood stains on it. She hadn't bothered to change out of it before falling into bed and drifting off to sleep last night. As quietly as I can, I rummage around in her pack until I find I fresh, clean, white pelops. I lay it out across the table in this cabin we are staying in near where we defeated the chimera. It was a gift from the dryads, to rest and recover in between battles. I pick up her golden laurel crown and set it on top of the dress. That crown has become synonymous with her name, and I daresay it looks lovely sitting on top of her curly blonde hair.

Moving slowly so as not to wake her, I pack up a blanket and some food, and slip outside. There is a trail from the cabin to a small lake that feeds the stream we camped next to when we were here mere weeks ago, though it seems longer than that. After we defeated the Amazons, we were sent to dispatch of an evil pirate that was plundering the coastline. We made swift work of him and all of his assassins. But with all of the fighting, we haven't had any time for me to properly court her.

While she sleeps by my side every night, we've only shared kisses, and I'm quite happy with that. We have a long way to go before we will be at a point to be truly husband and wife, and it will be worth the time it takes to really get to know each other. I find a clear spot of beach and lay the blanket out on the ground. I produce some fruits and cheeses from the basket I grabbed and lay out a nice breakfast for the two of us. Hopefully Nike will wake up soon and find my note to join me. The sun hasn't risen entirely, and I don't want her to miss the beautiful sunrise over the lake.

It doesn't take long before I hear her footsteps down the path. "What is all this?" She asks with a smile.

"Breakfast! I thought you might want to watch the sunrise with me."

"This looks wonderful," she beams as she sits next to me on the ground.

I awkwardly shove a handful of wildflowers I picked that Kraneia pointed out that Nike might like to her right as reaches for some food. "Well, this was supposed to be a nice, romantic date, but I fear I just ruined it," I groan as I attempt to brush some honey off of the flowers.

"It's not ruined! Thank you, for all of this."

She leans against my side, and I put my arm around her. And together we watch the sky turn a myriad of pinks and purples, eating small honey cakes and cheese. There may be a lot of battles in our future, but I look forward to all of the little quiet moments with her.

Glossary

Glossary

Xiphos: a short, double-edged ancient Greek sword that was usually wielded one-handed.

Podes: Ancient Greek measurement, the plural of *pous* which is roughly one foot.

Sibyna: Ancient Greek spear used for hunting.

Teganites: an Ancient Greek pancake.

Tetartemorion: the smallest Ancient Greek coin.

Stadion: an Ancient Greek unit of measurement that ranges from 150-210 meters, or approximately 600 feet.

Palaiste: an Ancient Greek meausrment of about 3 inches.

Acknowledgement

This book has been a challenge to write, as I wrote it while being a momma to an infant. I have to say that I am proud of the fact that I got it done. I guess moms really do have superpowers.

All the thanks goes to God for giving me the ability to write. He saved me through His son, Jesus, and it is because of Him that I have hope and salvation.

Thank you to Jes Drew for putting together this multi-author series, and for inviting me to be a part of it! And to my fellow authors, we did it!

To my best friend Leslie, thank you for your encouragement in getting this book done.

To my husband, Dean, for helping me out with the baby while I worked hard to get this book done.

And to my readers, I hope you enjoyed this short story and my take on Bellerophon and Pegasus, even though it is in no way perfectly accurate to the actual myth. Stay tuned for a bonus epilogue coming in the near future!

About the Author

Britt Richards grew up in a close-knit family in a small Oregon town. From the beginning, her parents instilled the importance and strength of family bonds. Eventually, Britt's family moved to Alaska. Here she met, and married, the love of her life, and gave birth to her pride and joy; her adorably sassy daughter. As a young mother, Britt obtained a Bachelor's degree in History with a minor in Anthropology from the University of Alaska Anchorage; which she followed up by a Master's degree in Education from the University of Alaska Fairbanks. After obtaining her degrees, Britt and her family relocated to the pristine shores of the beautiful Lake Erie in Northern Ohio, where she currently resides.

Britt is a self-proclaimed bibliophile who gained a love and panache for writing in high school. Writing would become a minor hobby as she entered college and pursued her true passion, history, and all things King Richard III of England. With the pressures of motherhood and college, Britt once again decided to pursue her beloved hobby of writing with her debut novel, *Pushing Through*. When Britt isn't writing or teaching, you can find her spending time with her family, whether that be a game night or something outdoors, or curled up with a good book and cup of coffee.

Currently in the works for Britt is *Unsuitably Bad*, the second book in her Black Death Mafia Series. She loves hearing from her readers! You can contact her through her Instagram: @brittrichardsofficial or by email: brittrichardsofficial@gmail.com

You can find all things Britt Richards Publishing and more on her website, www.plague-poppy-books.square.site

Other Books by Britt Richards

Other Books by Britt Richards

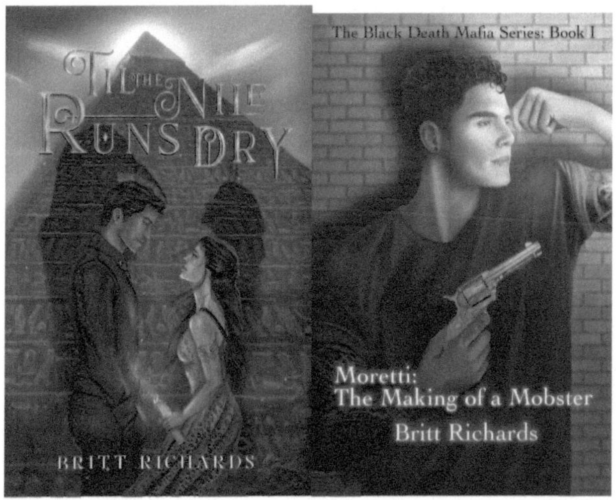
TIL THE NILE RUNS DRY
BRITT RICHARDS
The Black Death Mafia Series: Book I
Moretti:
The Making of a Mobster
Britt Richards

www.ingramcontent.com/pod-product-compliance
Lightning Source LLC
LaVergne TN
LVHW090532110826
845146LV00003B/1070

* 9 7 9 8 2 3 4 0 2 6 0 1 9 *